Eduardo lifted away from the door and walked toward her with long, easy strides that belied the speed and strength she knew he had. And his expression was too leashed to be anything but assuring.

This wasn't the suave, gleaming-eyed Prince Charming who the public adored, this was a carved-from-granite, coldly angry stranger. This was a side of him Stella had never seen.

Yet now, despite his iciness, that sensual intensity still emanated from every inch of him. And in seconds she was so close to succumbing to it again.

And that scared her more than anything.

He walked closer, his gaze never leaving her face, restraint evident in his too-measured movements and the compression of his mouth. But for a second he'd looked *furious*.

It was only with supreme self-discipline that she suppressed the instinct to step back. Just beneath her skin her blood simmered, almost humming in delight from his nearness. It was insane, and she hated her foolishness. How could she be so weak when the result of this want had just ruined her world? Yet that willful, wicked, reckless part of her only wanted him to *touch* her again. Touch her and make her forget the world as he'd done so easily once before.

Mercifully he didn't. He stopped a single pace away, his muscles taut, his stance wide and predatory—as if he suspected she might try to escape any second.

"Stella Zambrano," he said softly, but through gritted teeth. His intense lazuli eyes sharpened, hardened, *chilled*. And his words stabbed. "Welcome to Segreto Reale. We will be married here tomorrow."

These powerful princes request your presence before

The Throne of San Felipe

Destined for the crown, tempted to rebel!

Crown Prince Antonio and his wayward brother
Eduardo have grown up in the shadow of the
San Felipe throne. Now, with their royal destinies
fast approaching, the rebel princes must
choose their paths.

They've always resisted expectation, so the
kingdom waits with bated breath to discover if
the San Felipe heirs will be dictated by duty,
or ruled by desire...

The Secret That Shocked De Santis
March 2016

And look out for:

Crown Prince Antonio's story

Coming soon from Harlequin Presents!

Natalie Anderson

THE SECRET THAT SHOCKED DE SANTIS

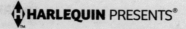

Recycling programs
for this product may
not exist in your area.

ISBN-13: 978-0-373-13422-9

The Secret That Shocked De Santis

First North American Publication 2016

Copyright © 2016 by Natalie Anderson

Printed in U.S.A.

Natalie Anderson adores a happy ending—which is why she always reads the back of a book first. Just to be sure. So you can be sure you've got a happy ending in your hands right now—because she promises nothing less. Along with happy endings she loves peppermint-filled dark chocolate, pineapple juice and extremely long showers. Not to mention spending hours teasing her imaginary friends with dating dilemmas. She tends to torment them before eventually relenting and offering—you guessed it—a happy ending. She lives in Christchurch, New Zealand, with her gorgeous husband and four fabulous children.

If, like her, you love a happy ending, be sure to come and say hi on facebook.com/authornataliea, follow @authornataliea on Twitter, or visit her website/blog, natalie-anderson.com.

Books by Natalie Anderson

Tycoon's Terms of Engagement
Whose Bed Is It Anyway?
The Right Mr. Wrong
Blame It on the Bikini
Waking Up in the Wrong Bed
First Time Lucky?

Visit the Author Profile page
at Harlequin.com for more titles.

For the fabulous Flo, thank you for being such an awesome editor and giving me such support—there'd be no book without you!

CHAPTER ONE

STELLA ZAMBRANO FELT as if she was sitting outside the principal's office, knowing she was in trouble without a clue as to why. All she could do was wait and try not to think the worst.

The military wing of the San Felipe palace was designed to impress and to intimidate. It succeeded in both. The vaulted ceilings were metres high, the floors tiled in a headache-inducing intricate mathematical pattern, and the walls plastered with gold-framed portraits of the De Santis predecessors—princes, military leaders, powerful men.

San Felipe, a famed island principality in the heart of the Mediterranean, was currently ruled by Crown Prince Antonio De Santis. Austere, yet beloved, and devoted to duty, Antonio was aided by his charming, utterly adored younger brother Eduardo. The public face of San Felipe, risk-taking, suave Prince Eduardo almost single-handedly kept the tourism industry afloat.

The most recent portrait in the vast room depicted the two brothers standing side by side in full military regalia. It hung on the wall directly opposite, dominating Stella's field of vision. She opted to stare at the floor. The sweat on her back iced. She desperately hoped the Princes were not present in the palace today.

'Lieutenant Zambrano?'

She looked up as her name was called.

'The General will see you now.'

Finally.

Stella searched the Captain's face for clues, but saw that if he were any more expressionless he'd be dead. She was uncomfortable, conscious that she ought be wearing her sharply pressed midnight-blue trousers and a starched white shirt, topped with her gold-trimmed blue jacket. Her brass should be gleaming, her ribbons immaculate, her star straight on her shoulder. Instead she was wearing sweat-stained fatigues and muddied boots.

She'd just finished her morning run when a stony-faced sergeant had appeared and said it was urgent and that she didn't have time to change. He'd driven her straight from the base to the palace, where the General of San Felipe's army had his official quarters.

Now she felt conscious of the marks on her clothing, the grime on her face. But perhaps the General would overlook her untidy appearance. Perhaps this summons was to give her the overseas mission orders she'd been waiting so long for.

But the unnatural silence spiralling in the waiting room warned her differently. This call was too soon after her last rejection. Too unexpected. And the carefully blank faces of the civilian staff present... The way they wouldn't look her in the eye...

Slimy snakes of doubt slid down her spine.

'Lieutenant?' the Captain repeated sharply.

She blinked, her brain lurching back to the present. Mortified, she stood. A superior officer had never been required to repeat orders to Stella before. She stiffly followed him to the large carved door that was firmly shut. He opened it and impassively waited for her to pass through.

Stilling her nerves, Stella walked into the room, then stood to attention at a respectful distance from the desk. The heavy door behind her closed with a thud.

The uniformed man seated behind the large desk didn't look up. He didn't tell her to stand at ease. Didn't tell her to sit. Didn't tell her anything. Instead he stared down at the personnel file open before him. She knew it was hers, but kept her gaze fixed on the wall behind him—yet another portrait of the Prince's. Peripherally she was aware of the man's greying hair and that he was wearing glasses to read the report. The General had been serving in this army for almost fifty years. Other men his age would have retired already. He never would. He was there for life. Because his life *was* the military.

She respected that. She understood that. Because she felt the same.

'Lieutenant.' He finally addressed her.

'Yes, sir.' She saluted.

He still didn't look up. 'On the afternoon of July the twenty-sixth you were based at the San Felipe barracks, is that correct?'

Her stomach dropped. That date was branded on her brain.

'I believe so, sir.' She licked her horribly dried lips.

There was no waiting now. Her instinct had been right: this wasn't the new mission she'd been hoping for.

'Did you remain on the base, as required, for all that afternoon and evening?'

She swallowed hard. It had been one hour. One hour in which she'd—

No. Don't think about it. Don't remember.

Calling on all her years of discipline, she blocked the memories from her mind, as she'd been doing almost successfully these past few weeks. But betrayal curled around her.

Someone had told.

'Lieutenant?' the General prompted. 'Did you leave the base without authorisation that day?'

These past couple of months her nerves had been at breaking point as she'd wondered—waited—to see if anything would happen as a result of that madness. But nothing had and she'd finally begun to think the danger had passed and that she'd gotten away with it.

She hadn't.

'July twenty-sixth,' the General repeated. 'Do you recall that afternoon, Lieutenant?'

'I…' Bleakly she realised she had no answer that she could utter aloud. She licked her lips again. 'I was nearby. I left the boundary only for a little while.'

'You were on call at the station. You did not have permission to leave the base.' A cold statement of fact.

She'd climbed down the cliff and gone to the bay, only metres away. She would have heard if the sirens had gone off—they hadn't. And she knew no one had come to her room for her because surely they'd have said something later? Wouldn't they have asked her?

'You had your routine medical check last week.' The General looked down at the paperwork again.

'Yes, sir.' Stella swallowed, nervy and surprised by the change in topic.

'Your bloodwork showed a problem.'

Problem? Edgily she waited, only just holding her silence, knowing her superior would inform her when he was ready and not before.

But she was fine, wasn't she? Fit and strong. Admittedly she'd been more tired than usual on her run this morning, but other than that—

'How long have you known you're pregnant?'

'What?' Stunned, she forgot to address him formally.

'A soldier on active duty cannot be pregnant,' he said crisply. 'You've not reported your condition to your superior officer. Another rule you're in breach of.'

Pregnant?

'I'm not...' She drew a shocked, shuddering breath. 'I *can't* be...'

It was impossible. There'd only been the one encounter in that one hour. And she'd used protection.

The General's already frosty expression turned Arctic, but Stella's blood had frozen anyway. No *way* could she be pregnant. It was the one thing she'd sworn would never happen.

He held up a piece of paper. 'The test was repeated with the second sample taken. There is no question of your condition. Do not make your exit even more ignoble.'

'My exit?' Uncaring of proper decorum, she grasped the back of the chair beside her, her head spinning.

This couldn't be happening. It couldn't be true. It *wasn't* possible.

'You are relieved of all duties.' He passed judgement in an expressionless drone. 'You went off base without permission. You concealed your condition. You are discharged from the San Felipe Armed Services, effective immediately. Upon your return to the barracks you will surrender the uniform you are wearing. All other property of the San Felipe principality has already been removed from your room and your personal belongings are packed. You will take them and leave the base. You will have ten minutes before you are considered to be trespassing and escorted off.'

Nauseating dizziness swept over her and the edges of her vision blurred. She was being booted out of the army. The only place she thought of as home. The only place she had to go. And she was *pregnant*.

Stella struggled to process the barrage of instructions. She couldn't be pregnant. Not by—

Bile rose, burning the back of her throat. Did they *know* who she'd met in that mad moment? Who it was who'd made her cast aside every inhibition as if it was as of little importance as a chocolate wrapper? Who it was who'd sparked that intensity and had her acting in a way she'd never done before? Did they *know* that she'd been the biggest idiot on the planet?

Pure panic threatened to derail her completely, but then her defences kicked in with a last spurt of survival instinct. She rallied, fighting to keep her thinking clear. To keep hold of her own future.

'Shouldn't I be court-martialled?' she asked, ignoring the catch in her voice and hoping he would too. 'Shouldn't there be a soldier present, recording this conversation?'

She did *not* want preferential treatment. Not because of what she'd done and who she'd done it with.

Or because of who *she* was.

The General muttered something incomprehensible. Not a regulation response. It was his first slip in this meeting—

a flash showing he might actually be human. She thought she saw a fleeting expression in his eyes before he looked down at her paperwork again.

But the expression wasn't the one she'd wanted.

'We thought it best to save your blushes,' he said curtly.

His abrasiveness dashed the last of Stella's hope.

Who was the 'we' who'd made this decision? And was it really to save her blushes? Or someone else's? Someone much more important than her.

Did they want this swept under the carpet and for her to disappear quietly? For this 'incident' to go away? For a moment rage blinded her. She wanted to scream this betrayal to the world. This unfairness.

But she couldn't. Because it was her own fault that her life had been totalled. *Her* poor choice that afternoon. But this preposterous claim that she was pregnant... It *had* to be false.

'I'm not pregnant,' she reiterated forcefully. She refused to believe it.

'You're dismissed.'

The blunt order stopped her cold. He'd made it clear her career was destroyed and he wasn't interested in her reaction or her defence. He didn't care. He just wanted her gone, quickly and quietly.

She stared at the greying, ageing man who wielded so much power. He couldn't know who it was she'd been with, because if he did he'd be angrier than this. He would care more.

Run, her instinct screamed. She needed to run before he *did* find out. Before anyone found out.

But she had nowhere to go. She had no permanent home of her own. When on furlough she travelled. Often on shorter periods of leave she stayed on the base and volunteered for extra shifts. So where? She couldn't go to *him*. And as for her childhood home...

She looked again at the older man who was now studiously ignoring her with that utterly impassive face. She tried to ask him. 'Sir—'

'You're dismissed.'

His emotionless repetition stripped the last veneer of confidence from her. All she had left was a plea.

'Father…'

General Carlos Zambrano, operational leader of the San Felipe Armed Services and Stella's sole parent, didn't respond. He merely put the paperwork back into the thin manila file that was all that remained of the military career she'd worked so long for.

She'd done the one thing she'd vowed never to do—had never done until now. She'd broken that barrier between professional and private. The barrier both she and her father had enforced.

Defeat twisted and she didn't try to speak again. Unbearably hurt, she turned and walked to the door. With every step she hoped her father would call to her. Stop her. That he would want to help her.

But he never had before, and today there was nothing but the inevitable disappointed silence.

Disappointment on both sides.

Glancing back as she closed his door behind her, she saw him still sitting at his desk. Still looking away. Still refusing to acknowledge her.

Once more she'd let him down. And there was no coming back from something this catastrophic. She'd never redeem herself in his eyes. She'd lost everything she'd worked so hard for.

She paused, clutching the door handle for support. She had no idea what to do or where to go.

Slowly she became aware of the surreptitious, speculative glances from the personnel working in the room. It was unusual for someone of her rank to be called into the General's office. They probably thought it was preferential treatment because she was his daughter.

But perhaps they already knew. That thought horrified her. Did they all know what she'd done and who she'd done it with?

And it *was* preferential treatment. She should have been dishonourably discharged or, at best, formally warned and demoted. Instead her father had used his rank to ensure her removal from the service was done in secret.

So there was no embarrassment for anyone.

Except she was left with nothing. No job. No home. The reputation she'd worked so long and so hard to build had been burned with the strike of a single match.

Everything was gone because of that one hour in which she'd lost herself. The one hour that no one was ever supposed to know about...

'I'm ordered to drive you back to the barracks.' The Sergeant from earlier materialised in front of her.

'Thank you,' she said, but the words barely sounded.

She sat in the back seat of the car and wound down the window, trying to get fresh air to clear her head. Her gaze skimmed over the grand homes, with their marble columns and gorgeous gardens, and beyond to the aquamarine waters of the glorious coastline. The beauty of the wealthy island now oppressed her. She willed the Sergeant to drive faster. She had to find a place and space to think. And that was not San Felipe.

Doubts and questions scurried in her mind. It was just over three months since that afternoon in the blazing sun. How could she be three months pregnant and not know about it? Horror filled her at the prospect—pregnancy had *never* been part of her life plan.

As soon as the Sergeant pulled up to the security station at the base she got out. No one came within sight as she walked to her room, but once she was there it was obvious someone had been very busy in that short time. Her space had been completely cleared. All that was left was a large duffel bag that leaned against the foot of the stripped bed. She opened it and her hurt deepened. Someone had taken methodical care to pack away her few personal possessions. It felt invasive and pointed—and why were the soldiers she'd considered more than colleagues so conspicuously absent?

Blocking the stabbing wounds and setting her mind to the task, Stella quickly phoned for a taxi to collect her at the gate, then stepped out of her drill uniform and pulled on the first things that came to hand—an old grey tee shirt, black yoga pants. She stuffed her feet into thin, flat-soled trainers. And she added a sweatshirt, because despite the early autumn heat she was freezing.

She left the clothing she'd removed in a neat folded pile on the end of her bed. Then she hoisted her duffel onto her back and walked past Security.

In and out in less than eight minutes. Not that her father was ever going to be impressed by anything she did. No matter how hard she tried.

'San Felipe airport, please,' she instructed the taxi driver, and slumped back against the seat.

A mere twenty minutes later she was inside the light, airy terminal. Stella ignored the award-winning architecture and walked straight to the nearest airline desk, requesting a ticket on the next plane out.

The airline attendant smiled and helpfully started typing, but only moments later confusion—and caution—lit her eyes. She kept on staring at her computer screen and tightened her grip on the passport Stella had handed to her.

'I'm sorry...' she said, then her voice trailed off.

Stella stiffened, casting a careful check about her. There were two uniformed soldiers in the corner. And another one heading her way. The Captain who'd been in her father's office.

'I need you to come with me, Ms Zambrano.' He reached out and took her passport from the airline attendant's hand.

Stella didn't move.

'Ms Zambrano?' he repeated quietly. 'This way.'

Not 'Lieutenant'. Not any more. Already she'd been stripped of the title that had taken her six years to earn.

She'd been rejected by the San Felipe army initially so she'd gone to New Zealand—her mother's birth country. As she held dual citizenship she'd been able to train there.

She'd worked so hard, risen through the ranks, until she'd been able to return to San Felipe with a record that not even her father could ignore. She was too good. She'd transferred, determined to maintain the rapid ascent of her career.

Now she studied her superior officer. Only he no longer had that role, because she was a civilian. He had no authority over her. And she could take him down and run. She'd had excellent training and she'd felled taller, bigger men.

'You don't want to cause a scene here,' he said, accurately reading her flash of rebellion.

Didn't she?

'I will carry your bag.' The Captain already had it.

She felt like snatching it back, screaming in defiance and stamping her foot. But it would get her nowhere. And the Captain was right—she *didn't* want to make a scene. She wanted to quickly skulk away and sort out her life in obscurity.

The airline attendant's brittle smile widened into an almost comical expression of relief as Stella silently fell into step with the soldier.

'You were at the palace,' she said, as they walked swiftly. 'At my f—' She checked herself. 'At the General's office. Why are you here now?'

'I'm following orders.'

'Whose orders?'

He kept his eyes front and didn't answer.

'Whose orders, Captain?' she asked again.

'This way, Ms Zambrano.'

It couldn't have been her father who'd sent him after her—he'd have said something back in his office. He'd made it clear he'd washed his hands of her. Which meant it was someone else making the call. Someone even more highly ranked.

If she'd felt cold before, she was hypothermic now. Underdressed and vulnerable, she missed the weight and strength of her boots.

The Captain whisked her through several security doors

and along a back corridor. The last door opened out onto the airport tarmac.

'Where are we going?' she asked, her apprehension growing as she saw the waiting helicopter.

'Somewhere you will be safe.'

Because she was under some kind of threat? 'Why wouldn't I be safe in San Felipe?'

'You were not planning to stay in San Felipe.'

No. She hadn't been. Another chilly finger pressed on her spine. 'So where are you taking me?'

But it seemed he'd used up his word allowance for the day.

The helicopter's engine was already running, the rotor blades whirring. Automatically she ran in low, and refused the offer of assistance from another soldier waiting inside. She knew how to strap in safely—she'd done it thousands of times.

Her bag was thrown in and the Captain pulled himself up into the seat alongside her, so she was boxed in by uniformed men—as if she were about to make a break for her escape.

Or as if she needed bodyguards.

She looked past the Captain to watch out of the window as the helicopter lifted into the air, her fingers curled tight into her palms. Didn't she have the right to know where she was being taken?

The men said nothing, but simply by watching out of the window she had the answer in less than twenty minutes.

Initially, from the air, the island looked imposing and inhospitable. It seemed little more than an oversized rock; nothing but sheer cliffs with jagged edges—a rival for Alcatraz. But as they flew closer she saw a rocky outcrop along the left side. It created a lagoon that harboured the smallest, most private of beaches. On the edge of that rocky outcrop was a tall fortress—a defence tower built centuries ago, to prevent intruders from entering the beautiful lagoon and disturbing those on the beach.

Looking back to the main chunk of the island, she could now see a large stone building. Before she'd only seen it in pictures, but she knew exactly where she was headed. This was the most private place in San Felipe. Access was forbidden unless you had a royal invitation. Because this was the island upon which the royal family vacationed in seclusion, escaping the exhaustion of their daily demands.

But this was no relaxed, simple holiday home. This was a *palace*, ornate and ancient, one of the many jewels in the crown of an island principality that had been celebrated for centuries.

The helicopter circled, giving Stella a perfect view of stone columns, stained glass, statues. The gardens surrounding the main building were large, formal and immaculate. Miles of hedging grew in intricate Renaissance patterns, swirling around rose beds and ponds. She caught a glimpse of a deeper blue beneath a stone archway—a pool. Another glimpse of something white. Her eyes were so wide they hurt, and there was a constriction in her throat that made breathing painful.

Most people would be thrilled to get a bird's eye view of this utterly exclusive island—and be beyond excited at the thought of setting foot on the place. Stella wasn't most people. Stella felt sick.

As the helicopter began its descent to a small helipad on the farthest reaches of the garden a loud drumming thundered in her ears. She couldn't tell if the noise was her heart or the helicopter, but it was growing louder, and her breaths came shorter. Her vision blurred.

Control yourself.

She tensed her muscles and mentally issued the order. She couldn't afford to be weak now. She had to be stronger than ever. She had to be the soldier she was and be ready to fight.

'If you would follow me, please?' The Captain exited the helicopter, hefting her bag onto his shoulder.

Well, it wasn't as if she had any choice. She quickly followed him along the immaculately tended pathways, feeling as if she was in the pages of a twisted fairy tale in which she had to cross an enchanted garden to find a beastly prince waiting for her in the castle.

Except he wasn't beastly. And that was the problem.

She wasn't led to the ginormous archway and large heavy doors that comprised the main entrance. Instead the Captain led her along a small path and then up a narrow stone staircase that took them to a wide patio that ran the length of the building. Large windows were set back from the uniform stone columns, and every so often formed a set of French doors.

Almost at the end of the building, one set of such doors was thrown wide open. Glimpsing a gloomy interior, she could see rows of bookshelves lining the walls.

The Captain led her right to the doorway, then turned and bowed. 'I will leave you here.'

He was gone almost instantly, his retreat swift and silent. He took her bag with him. And her passport.

Stella paused, unwilling to take the fateful step inside. She knew that Prince Eduardo De Santis would be waiting for her in that room. The piratical playboy Prince, the handsome patron of all things adventurous and glamorous in San Felipe. Capricious, spontaneous, spoiled.

Everything she wasn't.

Yet he was her one spectacular mistake. Her one tryst. The one thing her supremely disciplined self had been unable to resist that afternoon. And it seemed she was going to pay a fearsome price for her moment of Prince Eduardo's kind of fun. So now she was more than wary. But, despite the time she'd had to prepare herself, she felt utterly unready to face him. She had no uniform to hide behind, no tactical plan to ensure she won this battle.

And it *was* going to be a battle—against herself as much as against him.

'Don't stand out there all day.' His voice carried through the open door. 'Strange things sometimes happen if you stay in the sun too long.'

It was part command, part dry warning, part pointed reminder. And just his voice had her reacting in ways she didn't want to. Memories flickered at the edge of her mind. Teasing and tempting.

She couldn't let herself remember. Couldn't let herself fall again. She'd lost too much already.

Prince Eduardo De Santis wasn't so much a ruthlessly wicked rake as a seductive buccaneer. He didn't leave masses of broken hearts in his wake, more soft-eyed smiles and 'if only he would' sighs. But he *never* 'would'—Eduardo was too much of a freedom loving soul ever to be caught fast.

For many, that was part of his allure.

No one had a bad word to say about him, but he was most definitely not all *good*. He did as he pleased, and pleased as he did. A lover of action and adventure, he was a princely poster boy for all San Felipe's outdoor amusements.

And didn't she know that fact *intimately*?

Steeling herself, she walked into the room, blinking to hasten the adjustment her eyes needed to make from the brilliant sunshine to this dim interior. Despite the spots dancing in front of her eyes she saw him immediately. And quelled her quiver. He was as devastating as ever.

Tall, with thick black hair worn slightly too long, adding to his air of unruliness. His muscled body was clad in a black tee shirt and black jeans. He looked like a special ops assassin— only his feet were bare, in that arrogantly easy way that was so uniquely *him*. He leaned against the closed door, watching her with eyes that shone remarkably blue. The exact intense hue of the lapis lazuli the islands were famed for.

That burning sensation curled within her. Her cells smoked at the mere sight of him. And her heart thundered, sending yet more heat around her body.

Always she'd thought him handsome. Any woman with eyes would. But the pictures online and in the papers and magazines never did him justice. In real life Eduardo was even more impressive. And the utter, skin-tingling thrill of being held captive in his sight...

Stella also knew the reality of his perfectly sculpted body. The glorious size of him. The force. The *skill*.

She halted her mind again. She had to regain some control over this situation. Over her*self*.

Her pulse skittered. Her palms dampened as nerves choked her. She couldn't control that slick softening deep within her.

How could a man just stand there silently, yet exert such power over her treacherous body? How could he, with just one look, render her mute and immobile? How could she still *want*?

Pull it together.

Because if that medical report was accurate there was something far more serious to worry about. Someone other than herself she had to protect. And Stella had been trained to protect and defend what was most precious. *Freedom*—of a nation and its people. Including its future people.

So she paused just inside the door and looked back at him. Keeping her distance. And her cool.

The long silence built even more of a barrier between them.

Her nerves stretched as each second ticked on. As he regarded her so steadily with those captivating, all-seeing eyes. As he waited.

'You can't just kidnap civilians on a whim.' She finally spoke, making a stand for independence.

'You're not a civilian.' His voice held condemnation.

He'd been so angry when he'd found out who she was.

'I am now,' she countered, every bit as pointedly.

Something shifted in his eyes, but he didn't answer. Didn't acknowledge what had been taken from her or that he'd been instrumental in that loss.

She turned and pretended to read the spines of the books on the nearest shelf. Anything to give her eyes a reprieve from looking at him. Her attraction to him was too intense.

Her annoyance grew. 'Am I a prisoner?'

'You are here because this is the one place where we can have privacy.'

'We don't *need* privacy,' she snapped.

She didn't want to be anywhere near him. Not alone. Certainly not on his princes-only island, where he'd probably brought a million mistresses. And she couldn't let herself think along those lines—couldn't think of him as a *lover*. Not anyone's. Least of all hers.

She wanted to get away from San Felipe all together and work out what she was going to do with *her* life.

The silence turned ominous.

She was acutely aware of him. All that was unspoken rose, unbidden. The memories she'd pushed back swirled closer, threatening to swamp her. She turned, tilting her head back to glare across the room at him again—in defiance and defence.

His expression was grimmer still. Stella quelled another shiver. She'd spent years working alongside fearsomely powerful men and she recognised that edge in his eyes. It denoted more than determination. It spelled ruthlessness—said that he had the mental strength to make the harshest, most irrevocable of decisions. This was not the teasing man she'd met that searingly sunny day.

'You have been dismissed from the army,' he said abruptly.

'Yes.'

'Because you are pregnant.'

His tone jarred, damning her with his certainty. And disapproval. Her throat thickened and clogged so she couldn't answer. She didn't know for sure, but in her bones she feared it. She feared his response. His retaliation. Most of all she feared her own future.

She'd been in some seriously dangerous situations in her time, but she'd never felt as afraid as she did right now. Nor had she ever felt so alone. She had no one to help her.

As a result, she was more than disarmed—she was emotionally disabled.

Her heart resumed that too hard, too loud thudding again.

She took quickened breaths, trying to control her intense physical reaction to this horror situation. Trying to deny that her extreme internal reaction really was to *him*.

He lifted himself away from the door and walked towards her with long, easy strides that belied the speed and strength she knew he had. And his expression was too leashed to be anything like reassuring.

This wasn't the suave, gleaming-eyed Prince Charming whom the public adored. This was a coldly angry stranger, carved from granite. This was a side of him she'd never seen.

Because when she'd left him that afternoon she'd not looked back.

Yet now, despite his iciness, that sensual intensity still emanated from every inch of him. And in seconds she was close to succumbing to it again.

That scared her too.

But she couldn't peel her gaze off him. Never had she met such a wildly attractive man. Never had she wanted a man in the way she'd wanted him. The memories she'd tried to bury for so long now burst into her shock-weakened mind. For a split-second she saw him as he'd been that afternoon, naked and slick and braced above her, his gaze brilliant and fierce, his body both punishing and protective, while she—

'Stella.'

Heat surged into her cheeks and she banished the scorching image—mortified that she could lose control so quickly. She lifted her chin, bracing herself—because that was a warning tone if ever she'd heard one.

He walked closer, his gaze never leaving her face, restraint evident in his too-measured movements and the compression of his mouth. But for a second he'd looked *furious*.

It was only with supreme self-discipline that she suppressed the instinct to step back. Her stupid body turned schizophrenic. Instead of freezing, she was burning. Just beneath her skin her blood simmered, almost humming in delight from his nearness. It was insane, and she hated her foolishness. How could she be so weak when the result of this want had just ruined her world? Yet that wilful, wicked, reckless part of her only wanted him to *touch* her again. Touch her and make her forget the world, as he'd done so easily once before.

Mercifully, he didn't. He stopped a single pace away, his muscles taut, his stance wide and predatory—as if he suspected she might try to escape any second.

'Stella Zambrano,' he said softly, but through gritted teeth. His intense lapis lazuli eyes sharpened, hardened, *chilled*. And his words stabbed. 'Welcome to Secreto Real. We will be married here tomorrow.'

CHAPTER TWO

MARRIED? STELLA LAUGHED. *As if.*

She was a disgraced soldier. He was a partying pirate prince. The idea of him marrying her was preposterous.

'Did you hear what I said, Stella?' Shadows darkened his blue eyes. 'Do you understand?'

Why was he talking to her as if she was a two-year-old?

'You're not getting married,' she said. He was a playboy. And when he finally settled down—at least five years from now—it would be with one of the stunning minor European royals with an aristocratic seal of approval.

'I am. To you. Tomorrow.'

She shook her head. 'There's no need. I'm *not* pregnant.'

He caught her wrist. 'Do not lie to me. *Ever.*'

She flinched, squeezing to stop her cells sizzling at his touch. 'I'm not.'

She couldn't be pregnant—surely she'd know if she was? Wouldn't she have symptoms? She struggled to remember her last cycle, but other memories—whispered mentions of her mother—crowded her mind. Confused her. Scared the hell out of her.

Her skin burned. The edge of her vision wobbled and blurred.

'You're saying the report is wrong?' he prompted.

'I'm saying I don't know.' She frowned, trying to focus.

'Well, *I* am saying that if you *are* pregnant we marry immediately. I am not having my child born illegitimately and left to live on the fringes of society, with none of the benefits he or she should rightly have.'

Royal benefits.

Stella refused to believe this was happening. She refused

to allow control to be taken over every aspect of her life. She'd find an escape. *Immediately.*

'Even if I am pregnant…who's to say it's yours?' she challenged, breathing hard to fill her constricted lungs.

Deadly silence followed.

His grip on her wrist tightened painfully, then he grasped her chin with hard fingers and tilted it. Defiantly she held his gaze.

'Try saying that again,' he muttered, through lips that barely moved.

She couldn't answer. She couldn't breathe. Her heart hammered loud and hard, as if trying to smash free from its cage.

'I remember,' he said, low and harsh and so very angry. 'I remember *everything.*'

They both knew the truth.

They'd both been aware of her feverish fumbling. Of her physical reaction—the resulting stain of surrendered innocence that couldn't be feigned. She'd been with no other man before and no man since.

If she was pregnant, Prince Eduardo De Santis was the only possible father.

'We used protection…' she whispered unhappily.

'It was *your* condom.' He suddenly released her.

His cool attack sent a sharp edge of alarm scurrying down her spine. 'Army issue,' she snapped back.

Issued years and years ago. And it had been in her wallet ever since—surviving heat, travel, cold, time. At least she'd *thought* it had survived those things. Did condoms have 'best before' dates? Dread washed over her—surely she couldn't have been so stupid?

'I didn't…' She breathed hard but her words remained a mere whisper. 'I didn't know.'

'You didn't know I was going to be there because *I* didn't know. Taking a walk on the beach that day was a spontaneous decision. An unfortunate one, as it turns out.'

Had he wanted to think she'd somehow schemed her way into this situation? But he couldn't. Because it was a spurof-the-moment decision of *his* that had caused this. As if she would ever *want* to become pregnant!

He watched her relentlessly as reality began to sink in.

She turned, breaking free of his intense gaze to stare sightlessly at the floor. She'd just lost her job. The one man she'd never ever wanted to see again was insisting she marry him tomorrow. And if she was having a child it would need shelter and food and warmth. If she was pregnant she'd have to do what her mother hadn't. She'd have to survive childbirth.

Her whole world darkened and spun.

With a muttered oath he grabbed her hand again and guided her a couple of paces across the room. She hated herself but her skin burned—her cells aching for his closer touch, for him to pull her all the way towards him, to tuck her against his body and press her close.

As if she hadn't got into enough trouble.

'Take off your sweatshirt,' he ordered as he pushed her into a large plush armchair.

'What?'

'You're flushed,' he explained dismissively. 'You need to cool down.'

He tugged at her sleeves. Stella quickly pulled away, slipping her sweatshirt over her head to stop him from doing it and humiliating her completely. Because the look in his eyes was controlled and blank. Unaroused. He didn't want her that way any more. He was livid and she didn't blame him.

She scrunched her sweatshirt into a ball in her lap and stared down at it, thinking furiously. She heard him walk away, heard a clinking sound. And then he was back.

'Here.' He held a crystal tumbler out to her. His frown deepened as she hesitated.

'It is only water,' he muttered impatiently, taking her hand and curling her visibly trembling fingers around the glass.

Stella sipped a small amount and determined to pull herself together and straighten out this mess. 'We're not getting married. This is another of your whims.'

'My whims?'

Slowly she nodded. 'Like seducing strange women on the beach.'

'*You* were the one swimming when you shouldn't have been. You're just as spontaneous. You said yes.'

'I'm saying *no* now. This is my *life*.'

'I am well aware of it,' he countered. 'It is not what I wish for mine either. But that is not the point.'

Stupidly, his words wounded her. *Yeah, this is no fairy tale.*

'There is a doctor present.' Eduardo leaned against the large reading table near her. 'He will examine you.'

'Pardon?' She nearly smashed the glass of water on the floor.

'A doctor. Your condition must be assessed.'

Here and now? He *had* to be joking.

One look at his implacable expression told her he wasn't.

Control over her life was slipping further from her grasp and her outrage over his high-handed treatment grew. She wanted to see her *own* doctor in her *own* time and in *private*. She straightened. 'I will not be subjected to this…invasiveness. You have no right.'

'I have every right.'

'It is *my* body.'

'And *my* baby,' he shot back.

'Mine too,' she whispered, suddenly afraid. So very, very afraid—of now, of what it might mean for tomorrow and for a few months' time.

Even assuming everything went okay, he had such power and she had none. He could take her baby and send her away if he chose. Banish her. He would be able to. He could sell the world any kind of story. He had such charm he could sell the moon and the stars to the heavens.

'*Ours*,' he answered, his tone more measured. 'But you were going to leave San Felipe. Why?' He trained his fierce gaze on her. 'Where were you going to go? What were you planning to do?'

'Nothing, I—' She broke off. She'd had no plan other than to get away and think. What did *he* think she'd been going to do?

She hated the look of suspicion and condemnation in his eyes. Why was Eduardo determined to think the worst of her?

'You did not turn to your father?' he said.

She'd tried, but her father had turned his back. And when the General found out the whole story he'd be even more furious.

'He's not pleased,' Stella mumbled.

Eduardo's nostrils thinned and he finally glanced away from her.

'He does not know who I was with,' she added in a low voice, her embarrassment excruciating. 'No one does.'

Eduardo turned back to her. 'You have not told anyone?'

'Have I boasted that I bedded one of San Felipe's princes on the beach? No. I have not.' Her flush scorched her skin.

'Your discretion is a credit to you.'

She nearly rolled her eyes. As if *his* approval was anything she wanted!

His intense scrutiny softened and he almost smiled, as if satisfied at something. 'You will see the doctor now.' He walked to the door, opening it and calling in a low voice.

Stella set the glass down and steeled herself. Were there other people here who *knew*? She'd never felt shame over her action that afternoon, but she'd wanted to keep it close—just her one private memory to treasure. But now the world was going to know how reckless she'd been.

'You feel unwell again?' Eduardo had returned to stand right in front of her, looking angry again.

'I feel shocked,' she corrected miserably.

She was angry too. Mostly with herself. That she could have been such a fool.

'Prince Eduardo?' A man spoke from the doorway.

'Dr Russo.' Eduardo turned so he stood beside her chair. 'Please come in. I'd like you to meet Stella.'

Stella didn't even glance at the doctor. She was too surprised by the charming, 'glossy-pages prince' look that suddenly lit up Eduardo's face.

'I understand there may be good news today?' The doctor couldn't quite hide the excited note in his voice as he quickly crossed the room.

'We hope so.' Eduardo placed a hand on her shoulder in a mockery of a loving gesture.

'That is very exciting.' The doctor smiled as he put his bag on the big desk and opened it. 'I'm sure you're desperate for confirmation, so shall we do that right away?'

The man lifted out a small box and turned to her, still with that smile. But his eyes were wide and sharp and *prying*.

'You know how to use this?' He handed her a commercial pregnancy test.

'Yes.' Mortified, Stella wanted to hide.

'This way, Stella.' Eduardo took her hand and pulled her out of the chair. He wrapped his arm around her waist and walked her to the doorway. 'There is a powder room second door on the left,' he murmured, but there was steel beneath the soft tone. 'One of my assistants will help you if you can't find your way back.'

This wasn't pleasant courtesy. He was issuing a warning. She was under surveillance and she couldn't escape.

'Why don't you just wait here for me?' she whispered back snappily.

'Good idea.'

He walked with her right to the bathroom door. For a horrified second she thought he was actually going to go into the room with her, but he paused and she shut the door in his face.

Her palms were damp and she grimaced, but the indignity of doing the pregnancy test paled in the light of what the result might show. In her heart she knew her army medical tests wouldn't have been mixed up. The San Felipe army was too good for such a mistake to be made. It was Stella who'd made the mistake and the result could be catastrophic.

* * *

Eduardo De Santis leaned against the wall and waited, furious and impatient that he'd found out so late. That she'd nearly escaped from the country. Where had she been going to go? What had she been planning to do? He couldn't figure it out. Couldn't figure *her* out.

She finally emerged and walked back to the library. She held the test tightly in her fist and wouldn't meet his eyes. Wouldn't speak either.

She barely came to his shoulder. Her blonde hair was scraped back into a straggly ponytail, her skin was shiny and her loose clothes old. He still thought she was beautiful. And dangerous.

She placed the test on the desk by Dr Russo. Eduardo watched as the result was revealed. It didn't take the two minutes it was supposed to. The word was illuminated almost immediately.

Pregnant.

The last hint of colour drained from her cheeks. Her lashes lifted and she looked up at him. The intense emotion in her expression struck deep and burned hot within his belly.

Stark fear.

She was *right* to be afraid. He'd never felt so angry— not since the last time he'd seen her. Was her wide-eyed, wounded reaction all an act? Had she somehow planned this? He knew that was impossible, but there was *something* he couldn't trust in her.

It took him a moment to simmer down enough to think— though he'd been doing nothing *but* thinking since his aide Matteo had phoned this morning, to relay information about a certain young lieutenant Eduardo had asked him to keep tabs on.

Inexplicably, as that burst of anger settled, another ferociously hot feeling surged in its place. *Satisfaction?* As if he

were some Neanderthal, proud of his success in procreating
and preserving the species—the family name.

His name.

But Eduardo did not have the same liberty as others. He
could not do entirely as he wanted. He was part of the royal
family and with that came restrictions, responsibilities and
requirements not to get in trouble. He was the public 'face'
of his country, and one day he would have to marry.

He was eighteen months off thirty. Palace aides had
been dropping hints about a royal wedding for the past year.
They'd even gone so far as to invite every European society
princess or supermodel to the upcoming annual autumn ball,
in the desperate hope that one might catch the princes' eyes.
They were dreaming if they thought *any* would interest Antonio. And if Eduardo had to marry eventually, what better
bride than the woman already carrying his baby?

So was it any surprise that the plan had come to him half
formed as soon as he'd found out this morning? Now it only
needed to be enacted—quickly, quietly, incontrovertibly.

He took her hand in his. Her fingers were freezing. Instinctively he tightened his grip and rubbed this thumb over
her knuckles.

'Darling,' he muttered roughly. 'I'm so pleased.'

Startled, she choked on a gasp. He leaned close and kissed
her temple, so his head hid her suddenly astounded—and
angry—expression.

He had absolute faith in the discretion of his physician, but
Dr Russo was also his brother's doctor. Patient confidentiality might not hold when it was the Crown Prince asking questions. Eduardo had to sell this as a love match—starting now.

When he drew back a flush of colour had returned to her
cheeks, but she still looked so slim and vulnerable.

He knew she wasn't. Those apparently skinny biceps
could support her entire body weight, and her legs could
wrap around a man and lock him in close. She was strong,
powerful, and he wanted to kiss her properly—her mouth,

her body. Latent and unwelcome desire rippled in his gut—like a beast beneath the surface of an eerily still lake.

'You are in good health?' Dr Russo turned to Stella.

Eduardo listened impatiently as the doctor asked her preliminary questions. He wanted the man to do his job, but he also wanted him gone so he could ensure his control over Stella and this situation.

Stella nodded.

'Do you have any idea of the date of conception?'

Precisely. But Stella didn't answer.

Eventually Eduardo did. 'Possibly late July.'

There was a startled look in the doctor's eyes as he worked out how far along Stella must be, but the man was wise enough not to comment. He kept asking his routine questions. 'You've had no morning sickness?'

'No symptoms at all. I have an irregular cycle,' she said in a strangled voice. 'Apart from that I've always been very healthy.'

'From your army medical file it seems that indeed you are,' the doctor said jovially, apparently ignorant of the tension swirling in the room. 'So there's nothing else—no family history that we ought to be aware of?'

Her eyes dropped. Inside his, her hand had curled into a fist.

'Stella?' Eduardo prompted, and felt her shiver alongside him.

But she shook her head.

'Good.' The doctor smiled. 'I'm sure you would like privacy to celebrate, so I will leave you with some information for you to read together at your leisure.'

A pamphlet didn't seem much for something so important. 'Shouldn't you do more tests?'

'I will arrange a scan to be done on the mainland next week,' Dr Russo answered. 'For now I'm confident that Stella can continue with her normal routine.'

Something flashed in her eyes. She knew she was never

doing her 'normal routine' again. Eduardo knew that her dismissal from the army rankled, but it was convenient.

'You may, of course, also continue normal sexual relations,' the doctor added as he closed up his briefcase.

Eduardo felt her fist clench again—in revulsion? Was she *afraid* of him? Was that why she'd run away that day? Why she'd looked so terrified at the pregnancy result?

He gritted his teeth and maintained his smile. 'Thank you, Doctor. I will be in touch.'

The doctor lifted his bag and his smile grew impossibly wider. 'Congratulations. This is a wonderful thing for San Felipe. The bells will be ringing loudly in a few months' time.'

Indeed they would. But first Eduardo had to ensure the legitimacy of the next royal heir.

He released Stella's hand to escort the doctor to the door, closing it firmly after the man. Then he turned and leaned back against it, waiting for her next move.

'I'm not marrying you,' she said firmly, rising from the chair to stand in the centre of the room.

'No?' He lifted away from the door and walked towards her. He was pleased to see her trembling had ceased. 'Tell me *your* plan.'

She stared up at him, not stepping back even when he stepped too close. Her serious eyes were fixed on his. Both her hands had fisted now. By sheer force of will he kept his own hands at his sides, not lifting his fingers to rub at the skin she'd marked that day on the beach. And as he looked down at her defiant stance the desire that had felled him that day returned in full force.

Even for him it had been shocking. He was known for his adrenalin addiction—his spontaneous decisions and risk-taking. In truth his risks were never that great, because he was too constrained by responsibility, but to have taken a woman he'd only just met...to have seduced her within minutes in broad daylight...? He'd not done that even in his most hedonistic university days.

She'd looked so stormy—strong and sensual. She'd waded into those waves without so much as a glance around or a second's hesitation as the cool water had hit her. She'd been every inch the fighter then. And she looked it now.

He didn't want children at this time in his life. Definitely didn't want a wedding. But he'd step up. Because there was an underlying benefit for someone even more important.

'Your plan, Stella?' he prompted, irritably ignoring the urge to haul her against him and kiss her into compliance.

She didn't answer.

'Why didn't you come to me?' he asked. *Was* she afraid of him? Or was it just the usual—no one thought Prince Eduardo could be capable in a crisis.

'I didn't know,' she said, as if choking on the words.

He wanted to believe her, and almost did. He even felt a twinge of sympathy. But he damped it down. People lied. People withheld information. She already had. This would never have happened had she been honest in the first place. But she'd hidden her identity for reasons he had yet to work out, and the fact that she had given her virginity to him so quickly was utterly unfathomable.

'Where were you going to go?' he asked, wanting to see whether she'd offer even a scrap more information.

'I don't know. Anywhere.'

Anywhere but to him. That was clear. And she wasn't willing to talk about it. Why was she so secretive? And why did he still want her so acutely?

He clamped his teeth together, angered by the searing betrayal of his body. She was just another woman, wasn't she? Hadn't he had plenty? But he hadn't slept with another woman in the weeks since that afternoon. Maybe that was why he was feeling the edge now.

He knew it wasn't.

'You have no choice, Stella,' he said harshly. This situation *would* be defused, because there could only be duty now. 'And nor do I. We must make the best of this situation. We must do the right thing.'

She stared at him, and he knew she was desperately thinking up alternatives. 'I cannot stay here.'

'You can. And you will.'

He didn't like the look that now entered her eyes. It echoed the way she'd looked at the result of that pregnancy test. Terrified.

'Think of it as a mission.' He softened, trying to speak in language she understood to reassure her. 'Like a tour of duty. It doesn't need to be for ever.'

And it didn't. While not ideal or desirable, a divorce within the royal family was something that could be weathered. An illegitimate heir, however, was not.

She stiffened at his words, the spark in her eye reigniting, but she paused before answering, 'I understand.'

He'd angered her, but at least that vitality had returned to her expression. His skin tightened and his blood heated.

'But now I've had a chance to think,' she said slowly, 'it seems obvious to me that we don't need to do this at all. Your brother is the Crown Prince. He makes the laws. So he can simply change the law to recognise the child as your heir. There is no need for us to *marry* for the baby to have its birthright.'

Anger flared. Would she deny his child? Would she defy him? And she dared suggest he ask his *brother* to fix up this mess? Never would he do that.

'My baby will have nothing less than she or he deserves. Nothing less than the very best.' He placed his hands on her fine-boned shoulders and spoke right into her face. 'I repeat. We will be married here tomorrow. Whether you like it or not, it is what will happen.'

She flung her head back and glared up at him. 'You can't make me.'

'No?' He laughed at the challenge, and the urge to bait her was irresistible. 'You are a soldier. You are trained to do as you are told.'

Her nostrils flared. 'I will not obey *you*. You are not my superior officer. And I'm no longer a soldier.'

'You're a born soldier,' he said. 'And I am a prince of the realm.'

'But not the Crown Prince.' Her eyes flashed. 'You're not the supreme commanding officer. You're not the monarch who passes the laws of the land. You are nothing but a mere man to me.'

His lips curled as satisfaction rushed and adrenalin surged, sharpening every one of his muscles. This challenge and fearless fighting vitality was what he'd liked about her. She was no prince-adoring sycophant.

'A man that you wanted. That you *had*. That you're now stuck with. For better or for worse,' he mocked, but he meant it. 'And you *will* do as I say tomorrow. You'll find you have very little choice in the matter.'

'There are always choices.' Her chin stayed high, her expression determined.

And she had made hers. She'd turned her back on him and climbed away. At the time he'd only been able to watch, angered beyond belief and yet frankly marvelling at her agility.

Then he'd waited to see what the ramifications would be. He'd ordered a trusted ally to keep an eye on her, because as much as he wanted to move on he couldn't until he understood why she'd done what she had. He needed to ascertain whether she would sell her story or try to seize some other opportunity that he couldn't foresee. But there'd been only silence. Until that call today from his aide—detailing the worst consequence ever.

'Some choices are wiser than others,' he said ruefully. 'Do not make this harder than it needs to be. There is no point banging your head against this particular brick wall. You're only going to bruise yourself.'

He leaned closer, so close to the tense, sulky mouth that he knew was actually soft and hungry. The mouth he wanted more than was rational. The mouth he would not let himself taste again until she acquiesced to everything.

Until he was certain she really wanted him again.

Because she was an enigma, this woman who'd given so much and yet held so much back. He did not trust her. But he wanted her. Her quickened breathing fanned his smouldering desire and the spark in her eyes ignited it.

'If you insist on doing so,' he murmured huskily, 'I will kiss your bruises better.'

Stella sucked in a shocked breath. Silenced. He remembered their stupid banter that afternoon on the beach? How could he make a joke at a time that was so terrible? He couldn't be taking this seriously.

Yet his words and his expression sent heat licking along her veins. Sweetness rushed south to where it would be needed if her body was to take his again. She couldn't breathe. Couldn't take her eyes off him.

His slight, set smile now faded. He was staring back—at her mouth. She yearned to lick her lips but knew it was her body attempting to send a blatant signal to pull him nearer, and she was resisting that instinct this time. She was not giving in to it again. That basic, carnal instinct had succeeded in what it had wanted. Procreation. The drive to mate and create new life. There was no need for her body to want his again.

Oh, but there was *pleasure*, her reawakened inner wanton whispered. There was all the pleasure he could give her with his lips, tongue, hands and—

'I suggest you freshen up and then have some lunch,' he said brusquely, stepping away from her in a quick, leashed movement. 'We have many plans to make and you'll need to be able to concentrate.'

'Plans?' she choked, determined to bite back the desire that he so easily conjured from her.

Because he didn't want this any more than she did.

'Yes.' He turned and gave her thin tee shirt and clinging pants a coolly ironic once-over. 'You'll need to choose your wedding dress.'

CHAPTER THREE

WEDDING DRESS?

Surely he was joking—trying to provoke. Stella refused to rise to his bait. She lost control of herself around him, and if she was going to negotiate a way out of this and stay cool-headed, clinical tactics were required.

'You have a room ready for me?' She locked her wobbly knees. She'd show no more weakness.

'Of course.' He walked towards the door. 'This way.'

Stella made a mental map as he escorted her down the long corridor and up a grand staircase. The palace had looked moderately sized from the air, but it turned out it was more of a Tardis—corridors, rooms, doors in all directions.

'Your suite is next to mine,' he informed her. 'You can find your way back to the library when you're ready?'

'Of course,' she muttered.

'There are fresh clothes in the wardrobe. You may choose anything you like.'

She sent him an appalled look. Did he always keep a stash of women's clothing on his island? His wicked look dared her, but she wasn't going to bite. *Yet.*

'Thank you.' She walked into the room, closing the door behind her with a firm click.

Like the rest of the palace, the room was large and beautifully decorated—muted colours, soft, plush furnishings—and cool and comforting. She turned her back on the large bed and opened the door to a private bathroom and leaned against it in relief. Sleek, luxurious immaculate—all white marble and edged in gleaming lapis lazuli. *Of course.*

She eyed the enormous claw-footed bath, but then spotted the large glass shower stall. Several shower heads were strategically placed to blast water from all angles. Sheer heaven.

She turned on the taps and stripped, then stepped into the shower, shivering in delight as the water hit her. Water had rushed over her body that day on the beach too. Cleansing. Cooling. She pressed her palm on her flat belly, still unable to truly believe there was a tiny life within. How could she not have known?

She'd been so busy distracting herself she couldn't recall when she'd last had her period. She'd deliberately kept a crazy schedule so she'd hardly had any quiet moments when memory could ambush her. But now she leaned against the shower wall and closed her eyes, finally able to surrender. No longer did she have the strength to battle back those memories.

Not now she'd seen him again.

Not when the ramifications of that day were so dramatic.

The floodgates opened and every secretly stored sensation, every muscle memory, every beautiful image burst into her brain. Unstoppable. Overwhelming. Sensations trammelled through her as she relived every minute.

Despite the glorious weather, that day had turned bad just after lunch. She'd been summoned by her commanding officer and informed that there was a peace-keeping crew being sent to a high-conflict area. And she wasn't going.

'You're not the right officer for this mission.'

'Why not?'

All she'd wanted was one chance to lead a team. She'd prove to them how capable she was. But the chance had never been forthcoming.

'Do *not* question the decisions of your superiors,' he'd answered bluntly. 'Not this one, Zambrano,' he had added more kindly. 'Maybe the next.'

Or maybe not. She'd been certain her father was blocking her progression, but knew she'd never challenge him on it. She'd just work harder, longer…and ultimately she'd win. Because she'd be so absolutely the best he wouldn't be able to ignore her any more. None of them would.

But frustration had burned at yet another disappointment.

What did she have to do to prove her worth and make him see she was as fine a soldier as the men he favoured?

Back in her barracks, her anger had burned hotter. She'd been passed over for so many opportunities. Sure, she'd had a few crumbs thrown her way, but nothing that she'd really wanted, and she was busting her butt every single day.

She hadn't been able to stick around the base in such a septic mood—she'd needed to get her game face back. So she'd left her room and walked out into the afternoon sun.

While she wasn't on active duty she was required to be available in case anything came up. But she'd known she'd hear the siren from the bay if there was an emergency. Which there rarely was. And just a short time out wasn't going to hurt anyone.

The base was situated on a cliff overlooking the sea. To a rock-climber it was a good challenge, because at the bottom of the cliff, hidden by a rocky outcrop, was the Cala de Piratas—a bay accessible from the other side of the beach only at low tide because of the treacherous rocks surrounding it. Tiny, beautiful, dangerous.

Stella had climbed down—out of sight of her superiors, away from everyone.

It was island legend that some of San Felipe's wealth had come from the pirate ships that had been sunk against the jagged rocks hidden just below the rough waves. That legend was embellished with the whisper that even the royal family had a rogue pirate in their ancestry. Tourists paid handsomely to dive and explore the various wrecks not far from the island's shores, hoping to find gold.

But they didn't dive here, the place at the heart of the pirate folklore, because at this bay there was a rip tide that not even the strongest ocean swimmer could conquer. Stella hadn't intended to swim—only to wash the sweat from her skin and cool the angry heat of her muscles. She'd kicked off her shoes and strode straight in, water splashing her shorts and tee shirt. But as she'd walked forward a large wave had buffeted her and she'd stumbled, almost slipped right under the water.

Strong arms had suddenly banded around her and pulled her back against a large body of steel. Hard. Forceful. *Threatening*.

Shocked, she'd jerked her elbow to free her arm and, moving on pure defensive instinct, turned and lashed out. She'd been trained well and her fist had landed true and hard.

She had heard his grunt and her own as visceral pain had zinged up her arm. She'd quickly flicked her fingers, reeling at the impact of bone on bone. But she'd drawn her arm back again, ready to land another.

But the giant who'd grabbed her had reached even more quickly, catching hold of her upper arm and twisting it behind her, pulling her harder, more tightly into his steely body.

'Stop fighting. I'm not going to hurt you,' he'd said, in a deep, loud voice right in her ear.

She knew her best plan was to go limp, then move and take him by surprise. But when she let her muscles relax and fell against him he pulled her closer still, locking her into a hold she knew she mightn't be able to escape.

It seemed he'd been trained too.

'You have a powerful punch,' he said.

Her throat clogged, but not with fear. She recognised that voice.

At three in the afternoon Prince Eduardo De Santis was wearing a tuxedo that was now wet to the waist. As the waves ebbed and flowed, the water moulded his trousers to his long, muscled legs and he was moulding *her* to him. Her wrists were bound in his broad hands and twisted tight behind her back, thrusting her forward so she was pressed flat against his torso. His legs were parted only enough to lock hers together between his.

Because of the motion of the waves battering them she remained standing only because he held her trapped against him. Because of his strength.

Her anger morphed into something far more dangerous. Far more tantalising. Far more foreign.

Stella didn't move. Didn't breathe. Didn't believe it. But that melting sensation deep inside her was undeniable. She'd had many hand-to-hand training sessions with men. All kinds of scenarios. She'd never become aroused by any.

'You're Prince Eduardo,' she said stupidly.

And while he might not want to hurt *her*, she'd certainly hurt him. Already the skin around his eye was reddened. It was going to result in a mega bruise. She wanted to curl into a ball and die of shame.

He inclined his head in acknowledgement, but didn't loosen his grip. 'You have the advantage. I do not know your name.'

And he wasn't going to. Her father would kill her. She'd be demoted in seconds. *And* she'd be a laughing stock.

'Why are you here?' he asked. 'This cove is not safe. Soon enough the tide will sweep back in and the sand will almost vanish. You'll be stuck here for the next twelve hours.'

A hitherto mute part of her figured that wasn't that bad an option if he was going to be here too...

'I'm sorry I hit you,' she said roughly, embarrassed at that rogue thought. 'It might sting for a while. Then it will discolour. You're going to be marked for a few days.'

His low laugh reverberated within her.

'You think I haven't been bruised before?'

Well, she'd never seen a picture of either prince with a black eye.

He smiled, and suddenly looked exactly as if he had a suave, dangerous pirate ancestor. 'If you feel that bad about it, you could always kiss it better.'

'I'm better at hitting than kissing,' she answered bluntly. Honestly.

She wished he'd release her. The waves washing against her were doing nothing to cool the embers igniting within her. So inappropriate. So reckless.

His wickedly blue eyes sharpened. 'If you kiss half as well as you hit, then I'll be feeling fantastic in a heartbeat.'

She shook her head. But tendrils of temptation unfurled low in her belly.

This was the playful pirate Prince Eduardo, who charmed and made women smile and sigh. And Stella was as susceptible as any of them. Truthfully, he'd always been her favourite of the two. A stupid crush held since her teens. It was the fire in his eyes and his daredevil nature that appealed to something within her own soul.

'Perhaps I should show you how it's done.' The smile on his sensual lips deepened. 'Or are you going to say no to me?'

'Does anyone *ever* say no to you?' she asked, sounding more scornful than she'd intended.

She felt the tiniest flinch as his muscles tightened that impossible notch more.

'Maybe I ought to be the first,' she added.

'You're telling yourself that I need a lesson?' he asked, the edginess returning. 'You don't strike me as a woman who'd hide behind something so obvious. I did not think you would be so afraid.'

His words heated her blood to simmering point. 'You think challenging me will make me say yes?'

'I don't need to challenge you.' He twisted to hold her wrists with just one hand, so that with his other he could trace the side of her face with a lazy, teasing finger. 'I don't need to do anything but be this close.'

'Such arrogance,' she said, trying to mask her breathlessness. But he was right. She was melting. 'You're risking another knock-back.'

She was used to soldiers coming on to her. And civilian men she passed when in full uniform. But in those cases it wasn't that they wanted *her*. It was about the power play— they thought she was tough and that she presented them with a challenge. Most of them only did it in an attempt to make her feel uncomfortable.

Eduardo De Santis didn't want to make her feel uncomfortable, or even to challenge her. This was basic attraction—raw and real and undeniable. Even she, as lacking in intimate experience as she was, recognised that this was a fireflash and it wouldn't easily be doused.

'You want to fight with me?' he asked softly.

Intuition told her there was more to his meaning, and the thought of physically sparring with him sent that slick of something hot and charged to her lower belly. She felt him adjusting his hold on her, as if he were assessing her strength.

'You ready for another black eye?' she parried.

'As long as you kiss me better everywhere you bruise me.'

Was he even aware he was holding her more firmly? More closely? She gazed into his hyper-alert brilliant blue eyes.

Of course he was aware.

'Naturally I would reciprocate,' he added.

'I don't bruise,' she lied.

'But you do.' He lifted his hand to her face again. 'I see them here. Bruises in your eyes. That's why I came in after you.'

She'd been so focused on getting to the water and cooling off she hadn't even seen him. She'd thought the bay was empty and she was alone.

Now she was alone with *him*. The most handsome man on the planet. The most provocative. And the only one to whom she'd had this kind of reaction.

She felt his body tauten, and hers softened as his erection pressed against her. But then to her intense disappointment he relaxed his hold, fractionally pulling away from her body in a polite action that made her grit her teeth. She *wanted* to feel his attraction to her. She wanted to know that she wasn't the only one bitten by this madness. Raw need snaked its way up her spine and clawed into every limb. She didn't want him to let her go. Not yet.

'I thought you were putting yourself in danger?' His voice had gone husky.

She was in danger right now. But she couldn't tear her glance away from his. 'I'm fine.'

But she wasn't entirely. She wanted him closer again.

'I'm glad.'

'You've ruined your suit.'

'And my shoes. And my phone. Indeed, the damage you've caused is significant.'

The desire to flirt, to play, to entice him as much as he was her, overruled her usual restraint. 'Are you going to throw me in a dungeon?'

'I'm giving the matter serious consideration.' He smiled, but watched her closely. 'This is called Pirates' Cove for a reason. Those rocks in the sea provide a thorny path to hidden caves once full of treasure... Not to mention the rumours of a secret tunnel connecting this cove to the island over there.' He nodded in the direction just behind her, to the small island reserved solely for the Princes' use.

He thought she was a tourist. Not surprising when her accent was not as strong as his. She'd spent too many years overseas at boarding school, banished from her home.

'Isn't that your private island? Where you keep your women?' Teasing him was irresistible. She could be a tourist for a moment, couldn't she? Not a soldier who'd promised to serve his family.

'Bound to the beds—that's right.' Laughter lit his eyes— and so did sensual promise.

He would, she realised, do just that. And, more appallingly, she would let him. She touched the tip of her tongue to her dreadfully dry lips.

'So you *are* a pirate prince? Is that why you're here— stealing treasure?'

Stealing hearts. He was scooping hers up without a second thought. And so easily he wasn't even aware of it.

'Who's the pirate really?' he challenged, gently shaking her. 'The mysterious woman in black? Strong, agile. Thief of thoughts.'

'Thoughts?' she queried.

'*Si.* I can think of nothing but you,' he admitted in a low tumble of words. 'I no longer care about what I should be doing. That I ought to be moving. All I can think about is…'

'Is…?' she prompted, melting.

He angled his head and finally pulled her that bit closer again. 'It is not right that your skill set is so imbalanced.'

She almost purred at the blatantly sensual undertone to his words, at the feel of his hard length pressing against her again. 'You're taking it upon yourself to rectify my training?'

'I think I must,' he murmured. 'Because if you know how to give a bruise, you must also learn how to make it better. It is only fair.'

He was wrong. Bruises healed just fine on their own. She'd never had anyone to kiss *her* bruises better. But she didn't mind going along with him for just these few moments.

'So what do I need to do?' she breathed.

'When a woman is bruised you must kiss her very lightly. With great care. To ensure you're not hurting her more.' He brushed his lips against her temple—the lightest kiss that made her toes curl into the wet sand. 'And you do this until you sense that she is ready for greater pressure.' He brushed his lips lightly over her skin again, then again. 'That she is ready for pleasure. And then you give pleasure until the hurt is forgotten.'

He claimed her mouth then. She leaned into it, letting him explore, and he did—with wicked skill, torching the tinder between them until white-hot need poured through her.

'Feel better?' he asked, drawing back, arrogant knowledge gleaming in his eyes.

'No. I feel terrible.' And she did. The yearning inside her was a pulsing, hungry thing that she feared would never be assuaged. 'Kiss me more.'

'Strong little thing, aren't you?' He half laughed. 'And demanding.' He suddenly lifted her, splashing back the few feet to the shore and setting her on dry sand. 'Well, so am I.'

'Little?' she teased, attraction magnifying her audacity. Since when in her life had she ever *flirted*?

He kissed her again in answer. Rougher—harder—even

more pleasurable. She sank into it, gripping him fiercely. She had no idea how long they clung, wet and wild on the edge of the sea. All she knew was that it wasn't for long enough. But he broke the seal.

'I want to see you bared,' he said harshly, pressing his hot mouth to her neck. 'I want to touch you.'

He was a man used to getting what he wanted. To issuing a command and having it obeyed instantly.

Stella was used to following orders. And this was what *she* wanted.

Heated and frantic, she knew she'd have only this one chance to feel this wild exhilaration. Stella wriggled free, pulled off her tee shirt and tossed it to the sand. Unclasped her embarrassingly utilitarian-style bra super-quick—before he had the chance to really see it and before she had the chance to think. And to stop.

All of a sudden she was there, half naked before him. For a moment he just stared at her bared breasts. She felt her nipples tighten, despite the heat of the sun and the warmth of the gentle breeze. Then he raised his glance and glared at her.

It was as if she'd been plunged into a crucible. Her bones became like molten steel. Malleable, she awaited his instruction. She realised vaguely that she would do anything he asked. And enjoy it. Because that was Prince Eduardo's absolute promise—pleasure, fun, abandonment.

She drew in a shuddering breath, startled at the ferocity—the foreignness—of her own surrender. And for a split second she froze.

His pupils dilated.

Before she could run he reached for her, hauling her back into his fierce embrace, kissing her with such a passion that her knees actually buckled. She looped her arms tight around his broad shoulders, kissing him back, revelling in the sensation of her breasts pressed against his shirt. She clung and she didn't care. Lust, savage and raw, overruled everything.

'What's your name?' he asked, his hands roving up and down her spine as if he couldn't get enough of the feel of her.

She didn't answer.

'I'm not going to let you go until you tell me.'

She didn't know what made her do it. Maybe it was annoyance at his arrogant assumption that she'd do as he asked— even though they both knew she would. Or perhaps it was the newborn imp within her, wanting to test him. She felt him tense again and her anticipation heightened.

'You *really* want to take some risks today,' he murmured. 'What else are you willing to risk?' He pulled her closer again. 'What am I going to have to do to make you answer me?'

'Your worst?' she suggested. 'Or your best.'

He stepped back and shrugged off his jacket, spread it wide and placed it on the sand. He pulled her to stand just in front of it, then dropped to his knees.

She stifled a gasp as she looked down at him. To have such a gorgeous, powerful man like this kneeling before her...

He smiled, as if he understood the riot of emotions plundering her nervous system—anticipation, disbelief, power, arousal. Before she could speak he reached up and cupped her breasts in his hands, and then bent forward to kiss her belly. She reached out and put her hands on his shoulders for balance. Watched. Felt. Trembled.

As he kissed his way across her stomach he worked her shorts down over her hips, taking her panties with them, until she stepped out of them and was naked. Her legs were quivering. She wasn't sure she could remain standing much longer.

He obviously knew, because he leaned back on his heels and looked up at her, his eyes very blue and wide. 'Lie down for me.'

He tugged on her hands as he spoke and somehow she just melted to the ground. He pushed her shoulders, pressing her onto his warm jacket. He knelt above her and kissed her. Starting back at her mouth, he kissed every inch of her skin, his fingertips dancing lightly, providing a teasing accompaniment to the pleasure of his lips and tongue. Her face, neck, breasts, abdomen, thighs... Slowly he worked his way down until she was twisting beneath him. Willing, wanting and unable to wait.

She arched up as finally he kissed her *there*. The erotic sensation of his breath against her core almost sent her over. Then his tongue swirled into her sex.

'You're so wet,' he muttered. 'And you taste so good.'

His hands firm underneath her, he lifted her to him. She didn't want him to stop because, no holds barred, he was all but feasting on her. Her fingers twisted in the hot sand, the granules slipping through her fingers, and she threw her head back, closed her eyes against the harsh sunlight. She arched, grinding against his wicked tongue as she teetered on the edge.

But then he suddenly broke the explicit suction. 'Your name, my little pirate?' he rasped.

She gasped. He had to be kidding. '*You're* the damn pirate.'

He fixed his mouth to her again and pulled.

Oh, please. Yes. Please.

Her eyes almost rolled back in her head.

But he stopped and asked again. 'Your name?'

'Don't stop,' she sobbed. 'Don't stop.'

'Tell me your name and I won't.'

'Stella,' she muttered. 'Stella, *Stella*.'

Her head thrashed as he went down on her once more. The unbearably blissful sensation hit, turning her sob into a scream. She roared her release to the sky and sea. And to him.

Long moments later she realised that he wasn't even naked. That he'd only removed his jacket. And now he was leaning over her, that smile in his eyes.

She sat up. Her fingers shook as a sudden ferocity overtook her. She needed to know him the way he did her. But the pearl buttons on his shirt were tough, and he laughed at her impatient muttering. Finally she spread it wide, and when she touched him he stopped laughing.

'That's it. Kiss me better, Stella.' He groaned, bending his head to catch her lips with his briefly. 'Make me feel better.'

Relief that this wasn't finished sent need surging through her bones. She didn't stop to wonder at his words. As incredible as that orgasm had been, she wanted more—and for once in her life she was getting it.

His skin was hot and smooth, yet she could feel the powerful muscles lying just beneath. The sprinkling of hair on his chest was a delight to her fingertips. She traced the path arrowing down to his waistband. She experimented, licking his flat nipple, teasing the tight little centre with her teeth— as he'd done to her. It had been such sweet torment, and she wanted to trick him the way he had her.

Suddenly it wasn't playful. It was pure animal passion. He might be big and strong, but she was agile and lithe. She kissed him all over, relishing the way she could explore him. Letting her, he rolled onto his back, pulling her astride him. She lay sprawled, intoxicated by a sense of power. Then she moved, kissing him to the heavens and back.

It was so *physical*. He pressed against her, grinding against her bared, open core. She pushed down to meet him, the rough, wet fabric of his trousers an almost painful friction against her flesh.

'We cannot do this,' he growled—a gravelly roar of frustration and anger.

'Why?'

He breathed hard, thrusting against her body. She couldn't help it—she writhed against him again. He suddenly flipped them both, pushing her hard into the sand. She moaned, aching for all that pressure—aching to feel him naked against her, pressing right into her and filling that gaping need.

A need that had never been as strong. A craving that had to be sated. Her desire had to be slaked. Desperate, she was driven to move, unable to stop herself arching. She'd do anything to draw him closer.

He growled again. Then jerked his hips away from her sinuous dance.

'I don't have anything, darling. I can't…' He groaned, straining against her for a heavenly moment. 'We can't,' he muttered in tortured tones. 'I don't have anything.'

It took several moments to register what he meant.

Protection…prophylactic…contraception… *Condom*.

She stared up at him, dazed, disappointment so bitter. 'I do,' she snapped as she suddenly remembered.

He stilled. His eyes burned into her with a look of such savage intensity she felt unable to breathe. Yet she felt bolder than she'd ever been.

'I have something,' she choked.

'Give it to me,' he ordered harshly, peeling away enough to let her reach for her shorts.

Her wallet was wet, and she struggled to part the old leather pocket and find the foil square that had been shoved there so long ago. They'd been issued with them back in basic training. Stella had stuffed hers into the smallest space and forgotten about it till now.

The flush built in her cheeks as she grasped hold of the small packet and suddenly balked. 'That is…if you want…?'

'If I *want*?' The short, tense laugh sounded torn from his throat. 'You have no idea how much I want.'

She gazed at him. 'Then show me.'

He stood. Slowly he undid his trousers, spreading them to slide them down his hewn legs. Her jaw dropped as he revealed himself to her. He was beautiful. Muscled, yet lean, his skin glistening and golden. And his erection…

She swallowed as he tore open the small packet and rolled the condom down his impressive length. The pirate Prince was so much more than she could ever have imagined.

That this was happening at all was crazy. But to stop it, to say anything, would be crazier still.

The hot sun beat down on her. The silk of his spread tuxedo jacket was soft beneath her. But all she could really sense was him.

He lowered himself over her, encompassing her world. 'You're ready?'

She nodded wordlessly.

He gazed into her eyes for a moment and then bent to kiss her mouth, then the taut tip of each breast. Then he licked her core once more.

She moaned, and tugged him to come back over her. It wasn't enough now.

'Spread wider,' he ordered harshly. 'You are small and I am…not.'

He pressed his wide palm against her inner thigh, pushing her legs further apart. He slicked his fingers through her wet heat. She hovered in a whirling mess of anticipation and need.

Then he rose right above her, settling into position, and thrust.

Stella sucked in a shocked breath. An incredible feeling of fullness engulfed her. He was so big, so heavy. She frowned, fighting the drowning sensation, crinkling her eyes to stop the smart of tears.

'Relax,' he murmured, pushing forward again. But then he suddenly stilled. 'Stella…?'

For a moment she couldn't answer. She was still breathing through the overwhelming feelings, riding out the pleasure-pain that threatened to consume her consciousness.

Oh, man. He was so very *much*. But at the same time she wanted *more*.

The whispered need spread like a vine within her, trailing hot spears of desire and sensation through her limbs. Into her soul.

'Stella.'

It wasn't a husky, swiftly murmured endearment—the kind temporary appreciative lovers spent like small change. This was a warning.

She felt his furious tension building.

Instinct told her he was about to pull away, but she was a fighter, and she was not having this end this way. Driven by an instinct she didn't really understand, she curled her legs around his hips, using every well-toned muscle she had within her to hold him to her and lock him in tight.

His rough groan echoed in her soul.

'Don't stop,' she ordered, in low tones every bit as furious as his. 'I want it. More. I want better.'

She *deserved* better. For once she was having what *she* wanted, and she wanted only the good bits. She wanted to crest that wave again, the way she had only minutes ago. He could help her.

'Show me how to ride.'

And then she remembered his instruction—to kiss it better.

The confusion and disbelief in his eyes didn't fade, and she couldn't bear to see a glimpse of hurt there too. Even though she'd given him her body, she'd held back something vital. That bothered him, and she was sorry. She'd kiss it better.

She curled her fingers into his thick hair and pushed on the back of his head, straining upwards so that her mouth met his.

It was the worst kiss ever. She banged his teeth and bit her own lip in the process. But she didn't stop. She refused to. And slowly her clumsy attempt grew into something more sensual, more skilful. Sexier.

His lips softened, his mouth opened. He let her in.

She made the most of it—tasting him, teasing with her tongue the way he'd done to her. Heat slicked her body again and she grew restless. The pain subsided. Now she only ached for him to move.

He tore his lips from hers and looked into her eyes for a long, silent moment.

'Please,' she whispered.

Finally his hesitation went up in smoke and determination exploded within him. He kissed her again. Holding the rest of himself still, he plundered her mouth. Then he moved fractionally lower, bracing and bending to kiss her puckered nipple. He scraped the sensitive nub with his teeth. An arrow of pleasure shot to her sex, making her slick. And at last he moved. A slow, gentle, rolling motion of his hips. Easily, his big body slipped slightly further inside hers.

She moaned. She wanted more.

To *really* ride.

But still he moved slowly. He teased a hand between them, rubbing around her most sensitive spot with torturously gentle fingers—just enough to make her scream. She was so close. So insanely close. But as he pleasured her, the desire to please him sank deeper within her. She wanted to know that he felt this magic to the degree she did.

She cupped his jaw. 'Eduardo.'

No matter that he hadn't given her leave to address him by his Christian name. No matter that he was a prince and she a nobody. In this moment there was nothing but naked joy. No past, no promises. Nothing but now.

She groaned. 'Please.'

She wanted him to move faster again, as he had before, when he'd been clothed and rocking against her. She spread her hands wide on his butt, squeezing the tight muscles, feeling the bunched strength of him slowly pumping into her.

It was so carnal. So delightful. Utterly unlike anything she'd known. And utterly addictive.

She didn't want it to end. Yet she wanted something more so badly. She wanted him to feel this completion *with* her.

She moaned in frustration as he kept the pace infuriatingly yet tantalisingly slow. She could no longer form words, no longer think. She could only moan and strive to kiss him more.

Finally he moved faster. His thrusts became rougher. He cupped her buttocks with both his hands now, holding her so he could grind into her as deep as he could drive himself. The hold plastered him against her, sealing them tight together.

She loved it. She met his thrusts with hers, over and over, their bodies wet with sweat now rather than sea water. Her fingers curled, clawing into his skin.

'Look at me,' he ordered harshly through tightly clenched teeth.

She already was. She couldn't look away. She'd never been able to look away.

His eyes bored into hers, their blue irises obliterated by passion-inflamed pupils. Only then her vision swam as her orgasm finally slammed into her like a wave sweeping over a rudderless yacht. She was capsized into a tumultuous sea of sensation.

His expression tightened almost to pain as he worked to hold his own release at bay. Instinctively she understood that he wanted to make her succumb once more before he did. But all she wanted was to feel his unrestrained passion. Somehow she had to summon it.

As her orgasm ebbed and feelings of bliss stole into every cell she fought harder, her fingers bruising, her mouth sucking, her tongue licking. She sought to touch him all over, to pull him over the edge with her. She poured every ounce of power she had into the passion she felt. Into somehow showing him what she wanted. And needed.

That was when she finally felt his massive body shaking—when his roar reverberated into her mouth as he gave in to it and released his hold on himself. His final thrusts came in a torrent of fury and lust. His satisfaction spurted. He shouted loud and rough, and sent her tumbling into the velvety hot darkness again.

He rested for only a moment. His breath blew hot and quick on her neck. Then his biceps bunched as he braced and pulled free of her embrace.

Suddenly empty and cold, she remained prone on the sand and shielded her eyes with her arm. She didn't want to answer the questions she knew he was going to throw at her.

But he didn't savage her. There was only silence.

Eventually she lowered her hand, forcing herself to look at him.

He was watching her face intently, and then ever so slowly he gazed down her body. The expression in his eyes was bleak and forbidding. She sat up, but it was too late to hide.

The smear of rust-coloured blood on her thigh was incontrovertible evidence. But he already knew the truth.

'Why?' he asked harshly.

She had no answer she could give him.

'You should have told me.'

'I didn't think it was important.'

'You did not act like a virgin,' he said icily.

'How is a virgin supposed to act?' she asked, every bit as frozen.

Shouldn't she have enjoyed it? Shouldn't she have pushed for all that she had? But she had enjoyed it. She'd been unrestrained, unfettered in her actions. And untutored.

She hadn't been *able* to control her reaction to him. She'd been utterly lost in that flare of desire for him. And she refused to regret it now. She didn't want him to regret it either. But it seemed he already did.

Before she could move he picked up her wallet, which she'd tossed to the side in her haste. Before she could think to snatch it from him he'd flicked it open, was reading her identity card.

The last of the delicious heat that had softened her fled. Dread solidified into a cold ball in the pit of her belly.

'Zambrano... Lieutenant.' He stood utterly still. 'No relation of General Zambrano?' He glanced at her, swiftly taking in her colouring, her features. 'His daughter,' he said brusquely.

He didn't need to look at her as if she'd done something wrong.

'You should have told me!' he suddenly shouted. Irate.

But if she had he'd have stopped. He'd have recognised her surname and refused to continue. If she'd told him she was a virgin he'd have stopped then too. And she hadn't wanted him to stop. She'd wanted this one thing, this one time, for herself.

But she hadn't stopped to consider the consequences—these appalling moments afterwards. And the possible ramifications for her career.

She hadn't thought he'd even notice her virgin status. She hadn't thought it would be so obvious. She led such a physical life she'd not really thought she'd bleed. And she hadn't thought it would really hurt like that. Nor had she thought it would feel that fantastic.

'Why did you *do* this?' He grabbed her arm. 'I *hurt* you.'

The bruise around his eye was livid now—but it was nothing on the anger *within* his eyes.

A good soldier knew when to attack, when to stand and defend, and when to retreat. There was only one option for Stella now. She jerked her arm—was surprised when he let her go. Then she turned and struggled to pull her sodden shorts back on. She pulled the tee shirt on too. She didn't bother with the ugly sports bra and plain panties, or even her shoes.

'What are you doing?' His voice was lethally quiet now.

'I need to get back to the base.'

'I will escort you there.'

'You will not. You will go…wherever you were going in *that*.' She gestured at the sodden sand-splattered suit now in a crumpled heap at his feet.

He glanced down and swore.

Stella turned away from him again—from the sight of him standing there tall and naked and filled with burning emotion. A crazy part of her wanted him all over again.

'Lieutenant—'

'No. There's no need to say anything.' She hated it that he referred to her by her rank now. 'No one will ever know about this. You have my word,' she said quickly, glancing to see his reaction.

He looked disbelieving.

'I don't kiss and tell,' she snapped.

'No, you just like to hit.' He drew a breath. 'And you are very good at it.'

'It's only a bruise. It will fade. There'll be no scar.'

But what about for her? She feared she'd just got a wound that would run bone-deep and mark her for life. She couldn't let it. She had to forget it. Her few minutes of heaven would be buried like a pirate's treasure, deep in the bottom of her heart and mind. Never to be found again.

She turned and faced the cliff.

He grabbed her arm again. 'You're not going that way.'

She shook him off. 'Watch me.'

She didn't know whether he did or not. But being partially dressed while he was still devastatingly naked meant she had the advantage. She ran and pulled herself up the rocks with a speed and nimbleness exacerbated by adrenalin and anger and the remnants of sensual energy.

When she finally reached the top of the cliff she didn't stop to turn and look. She just ran back to the base, the need for a fast escape driving her. Before she did something even more stupid like turning back and begging to see him again.

But he'd called after her.

'Stella? *Stella!*'

Even months later she heard him calling. As much as she'd tried to forget him—forget that whole afternoon—when she closed her eyes she always heard his furious demand.

'*Stella!*'

She frowned as she heard banging, then an ear-splitting splintering sound. She opened her eyes in time to see the door smashed open. Abruptly she was yanked back from memory into the present. Into the bathroom at the Palacio de Secreto Real. Where she was no longer alone in the shower.

Eduardo De Santis had been hollering her name here and now—and he was incandescent.

'What the *hell* have you been doing all this time?' His chest rose and fell, his muscles bunched from the effort of breaking down the bathroom door.

He stepped right into the stall and flicked the shower lever with a sharp, vicious movement, shutting off the jets of steaming water. But it was too late. His tee shirt was already wet. So were his jeans.

Memory melded with the present moment and she was speechless. Melting. *Crazy.*

'Are you unwell? Did you almost faint again?' He towered over as he interrogated her. 'Stella?'

Dumbfounded, she stared up at him, registering his frown, his concern, his confusion. His fury.

Once more she was *fascinated*. He was magnificent. Mesmerising. And *so* mad with her.

Suddenly she was furious too. With her situation. With him. With her stupid lust-lost self. And she was too shocked, too ripped open, too angry to do anything but answer with an honest snarl.

'I forgot, okay? I *forgot*.'

CHAPTER FOUR

'FORGOT WHAT?' EDUARDO PRESSED his palms hard on the wall either side of her—imprisoning her, uncaring about impropriety. But it was better than grabbing her shoulders and shaking her. He needed to see she was okay and hear her say it.

Her pale blue eyes widened. Deepened. But she didn't answer.

His heart thundered a furious tattoo. His muscles coiled as adrenalin streamed through his veins. He'd pounded that damn bathroom door for ages, imagining her to be unconscious and drowning or worse.

Reality was no less of an attack on his system.

Her lithe body was gloriously naked. Droplets of water glistened on every inch of her, as if she'd been dipped in diamonds. Dazzling perfection, her effect on him was akin to sorcery.

He forgot everything. To breathe. To think. To move.

The dazed look in her eyes mesmerised him. When he'd parted her thighs with his and pushed into the heart of her scorching heat she'd looked at him like this.

'Stella...' he muttered.

Still wordlessly casting her spell, she stared back up at him, a stormy, mouthwatering mix of softness and strength, all feminine sensuality. He fought back the urge to press his lips to hers.

He'd been unable to forget her energy and demand and passion that day. But afterwards she hadn't just left. She'd *run*. The only lover who had. Eduardo was the one to end any liaison—gently but efficiently.

Tendrils of doubt had wormed in after her determined, hasty departure, bringing a hint of unwanted regret. He'd damn well *tried* to forget, but she'd lurked in the sea of his sleep, calling like a Siren. He envisaged every intimacy, pleasuring her beyond endurance, hearing her, tasting her, claiming her, over and over again. To his extreme annoyance he'd dreamt of her every single night since that day.

Filthy, soul-scorching dreams.

Never had he dreamt of a woman the way he had of her. Yet memory had served him poorly. In reality she was more vibrant, more luminous than any fantasy. The electrifying *want* within him was intolerable.

'What did you forget?' he snapped, whipping his vocal cords into action.

'What are you doing in here?' She tilted her chin.

Glimmering energy arced, zinging back and forth between them—desire, shock, anger.

'Why didn't you answer me?' he countered.

'You didn't have to break down the door.' Her cool voice belied the heat in her eyes.

'You didn't answer me.' He measured his breathing, refusing to lose control, but temptation burned, stoked by her icy defiance.

'I didn't hear you.' Sharper. Hotter.

His frown deepened. That wasn't what he'd meant. He still wanted to know what it was she'd forgotten.

'You were worried about me?' Disbelief sparkled in her eyes.

'Is that such a surprise?' An hour ago she'd looked pale and scared. She looked neither now. 'I was bringing you a tray of food.'

'I didn't ever imagine you in the role of delivery boy,' she said.

'How *did* you imagine me?' He smothered his smile of pleasure at her weak attempt to put him in his place.

Her eyes flashed.

'You can strike better than that,' he added, in a deliberately provocative whisper.

'We both know I can. But are you sure you want me to?' she asked, her voice huskier.

Oh, yes—he wanted. 'If you're going to mark me, don't make it my face. There were too many awkward questions last time.'

She drew in a sharp breath. Good. He'd got to her.

But she stepped up to the mark again. 'If I hit you now, your soldiers would be here in a second.'

He smiled at her naïveté. 'They're under orders not to disturb me. I don't need anyone's help to handle *you*.'

Another flash lit her eyes. Another surge of adrenalin hit him.

'Handle me?' she snapped back. 'Like I'm some dog that needs obedience training?'

She did need training. And it would be her choice of carrot or stick. He smiled at the possible interplay, given her unpredictability.

Having the fine-boned creature of so many dreams finally in front of him, he realised how much he'd thought of her over the last few weeks. How much she intrigued him.

'Why did you do it?' Not the question he'd been going to ask. He didn't want her to know he'd spent so long wondering.

Her lashes lowered, veiling the blue, but she wouldn't lower her guard. She wouldn't tell him the truth.

Why the stab of disappointment? Why would he expect otherwise? No one opened up and confided in him. Not even those he cared most about. Especially not them.

In turn, Eduardo knew he couldn't count on other people unless he paid them very well. That unpalatable truth came with being a prince. Loyalty to royalty was a thing of the past. Most people now were out for what they could get— fame and fortune. Both could be attained via a connection with him. And that was all he really had to offer—palace life, wealth, but no real power. No real purpose.

But riches and recognition were enough reward for some. He'd underestimated that particular hunger before and he wouldn't make that mistake again. Instead he'd ensure that Stella was satisfied. She might not have told anyone about their tryst on the beach that day, but she'd not come to him when she'd realised the consequences either. Who knew what she'd been planning to do?

It no longer mattered. He'd buy both her silence *and* her obedience.

She'd be happy with the deal—he just needed to get it done before Antonio found out and tried to interfere. As it was, his brother would be highly suspicious of Eduardo's sudden 'illness', which had forced him to cancel all his public engagements for the next few days and withdraw to Secreto Real to recuperate. Eduardo had cancelled only one engagement in his life. The afternoon he'd met Stella.

He'd not gotten a woman pregnant before her either.

'Why did you do it?' He wasn't moving until she answered.

For a long moment there was only silence and steam.

'Why *wouldn't* I want to experience the best that San Felipe has to offer?'

She still didn't look at him—at least not higher than his chest. *Was* it just the fantasy she'd wanted? Unrestrained sex in the surf with the playboy Prince?

Disappointment bit harder.

He'd never wanted to be the daredevil spare heir boring cliché. He'd striven to shake it off, initially indulging in the idealistic, ultimately unrealistic ambition of studying law. Then he'd tried the military, only to be thwarted there too.

The lovely Stella's father had ruled out any possibility of Eduardo actively serving. He'd argued that it would cost too much to protect Eduardo, and any 'value' Eduardo might bring to the battalion would be outweighed by the risk to other soldiers' lives. Securing Eduardo's presence would take up too much resource.

In short, he wasn't worth it because his princely title was too precious.

Antonio had sided with the General. In a five-minute,

one-sided conversation they'd resigned him to a life of 'leisure', reduced to playing tourist in his own country. But, as so many citizens depended on the tourist industry for their economic survival, Eduardo did his very best—as he did in everything. But he did not particularly like General Carlos Zambrano.

As for his daughter...

She'd been absent from the General's palace apartment for years, else Eduardo would have noticed her flaxen hair and her athletic, curved figure so much sooner. She'd been in New Zealand—schooled there, trained there. Yeah...thanks to his security department he knew all the facts, but the dossier they'd prepared didn't give the detail he *really* wanted.

'Just the once was enough for you?' he asked.

She flicked the quickest of glances up. 'As it was for you.'

Eduardo watched as a pink tide flowed over her cheeks, and unexpected emotion glinted before she swiftly lowered her lashes again. Clenching her jaw, she remained silent. Suddenly so determined not to respond.

He drew a soft breath and pushed harder against the shower wall to expend the energy threatening to burst through his skin. Did she doubt that he was still hot for her? Primal satisfaction ignited his fighting spirit. But this beautiful warrior woman did not want to admit her attraction to him.

Why didn't she want to give in to it again when it would make this nightmare so much more bearable? Their chemistry had been—still was—incredible. He knew to his bones how good it would be when she was exactly where he needed her.

In her white dress, with his ring on her finger, in his bed. Not a minute before.

'I don't think once was enough,' he said softly, unable to resist teasing her.

'You never date a woman for more than a couple of nights.' Her eyes flashed fire. 'Am I not just like all the others?'

There hadn't been *that* many others in recent years. Now

he was more play*ful* than playboy—lots of flirt, little follow-through. It was safer when he knew how little he could trust.

Now her hint of jealousy fanned the inferno building within him. Sexual intensity almost overpowered him. He tried not to lower his gaze and drink in her bared beauty, but there were those dusky, tight nipples and the rounded breasts, the tight, flat abs, the tempting thatch of hair at the apex of her thighs, those dazzling droplets of water all over her.

He wanted to feel her flush against him. He'd have to rip off his saturated shirt and jeans, though, and they were sticking so tight it would take too long, and he needed to feel her *now*—

'As you can see—' she interrupted his derailed thoughts with a voice slathered in sarcasm '—I'm perfectly fine. So you don't need to *worry*. You can leave now.'

His gaze shot back to hers and his face heated. *So* caught. But she thought she could order him out...?

Eduardo was used to getting his own way. And he'd get it this time, because he was *sure* she was feeling this too. On an angry, lust-driven impulse he slowly, deliberately lowered his gaze again, blistering his senses, blatantly looking his fill at her jaw-droppingly gorgeous body.

He watched a trickle of water run from her hair to her skin, down the crest of her breast to her nipple, forming a drop there. His mouth was dry as dust and he craved a lick. Just one. Just one kiss.

His erection strained against his zipper. Lust clamoured a shrill mantra—*kiss, kiss, kiss...*

She quivered, the merest movement, as he ate her with his eyes, but she remained silent. Defiantly holding her head high.

Along with lust and need, another emotion snaked out from his gut—admiration. Then respect. And then regret.

What was he *doing*, standing over her like this? Invading her personal space? She was in the *shower*, for heaven's sake.

She wasn't going to let him intimidate her, let her nudity

be a vulnerability. She was all armour. Even when naked she was stiffened with pride and rebellion and courage.

He wanted her. But more than that he wanted her to come to him—as willing and as tempting as she'd been that day on the beach.

'Why did you run away afterwards?' Why hadn't she come to him to tell him she was pregnant?

Her lips parted, her mouth forming a wordless 'oh' while her anger burned brighter, melting into something else. But still she gave no damn answer.

That old disappointment was like salt in a freshly opened wound. But he didn't move—he'd never been so focused on a woman, never spent so much effort trying to read what he could from the few physical signs she couldn't help giving away.

Her hands were fisted at her sides. She was expending a lot of energy so as not to move. Just as he was. What didn't she want to let herself do? Was she, like he, fighting the urge to reach out and touch? Or did she really want to fight, then flee?

On paper she appeared the perfect obedient soldier. Until that afternoon with him she'd not put a foot wrong—never left base without authorisation, never fraternised. No boyfriend. No parties. No fun.

She'd never had sex before either. Which he guessed meant she was not a natural hedonist. Sure, she'd gone full throttle once she'd let herself off the leash, but maybe the intensity had been too much for her?

It almost had been for him. Goosebumps still riddled his skin when he thought of it, and *he* was used to sex. She wasn't. Had she been shaken emotionally? Had he hurt her that way? Was she afraid of him?

Suddenly he didn't want to know any more. He wasn't a man who could offer emotional support. He'd tried. He'd failed. More than once.

Stella wasn't the first person *not* to turn to him in a time of crisis.

'Eat the food I have brought,' he growled, pushing away from the shower wall and forcing himself to step away from her.

He ignored the thunderclap of fury from the lust clouding his mind, urging him to stay and press closer. He wanted to make her feel so damn good she wouldn't be able to stop pleading with him to do it again. But he was going to have to wait a bit longer for that little ego trip. Just till tomorrow.

'Make yourself presentable,' he said curtly, picking up one of the large white towels from the gleaming gold rail. 'I will see you in the library.'

She snatched the towel he rigidly held out and wrapped it around her, hiding her delectable body from his ravenous eyes, leaving him immensely relieved. And viciously frustrated.

Angered with his fixation, he strode away. 'Be quick.'

CHAPTER FIVE

STELLA FELT LIKE taking at least two hours, except years of drills and discipline overruled the petty desire to prove a point. She glanced at the treat-laden tray he'd carried to her room but her stomach was too knotted for her to attempt eating. She opened the door to the walk-in wardrobe and stared. Tags still hung on some items, and they were the right sizes and everything. Did he know her every personal detail? Damn army records.

Well, she wasn't wearing anything he provided. She had pride.

She dressed in less than five minutes, dragging on her jeans again, pulling out a different tee shirt from further down her duffel bag. Then she laced up her trainers. She didn't care what his idea of 'presentable' was.

But adrenalin scoured her veins. Her body knew she was in danger. Because what she'd forgotten—what she'd refused to admit aloud—was his *impact*.

That he could have her forgetting all her hard-earned rights in a heartbeat. She'd wanted to lean back against the wall and let him do whatever he pleased with her. She'd wanted him to be as naked as she. All he had to do was *look* and in seconds she'd been aching for his touch...

She'd been around hundreds of men all her life. Men more muscled. Men taller, broader, faster. Never had she been tempted the way that Eduardo tempted her.

Her weakness infuriated her. Could she *really* be this shallow? Could her head be so turned just because he was a prince? But she didn't feel this for Crown Prince Antonio, and wasn't he the more powerful of the two? No, it was only Eduardo and his irresistible smile, who devastated her.

How quickly she'd fallen under his spell. How easily he'd

seduced her. And he could do it again in seconds. He almost had in that hot shower stall. And she couldn't let him. Not now there was so much more at stake. She had to keep her head and carve out the right solution for this situation.

A wedding wasn't it.

She dropped to the floor and executed twenty press-ups just to expend some of the energy rioting within her. He'd wanted to know why she'd done it, but she could never admit that she'd long harboured a crush on him, or that he'd represented the kind of free-loving fun she'd never had. She'd wanted one moment just for herself.

She wasn't admitting that dreary little dream to him.

Quickly, quietly, she walked back to the opulent library.

As she neared the large doorway she moved more stealthily. Maybe she'd hear something interesting—

'Come in, Stella.'

Grimacing, she moved into the doorway and found him just inside it. His gaze skittered down her clothing. The skin about his mouth and eyes tightened. Yeah, not exactly 'presentable'.

But he'd changed too—black jeans again, white tee. Designer casual as opposed to her dumpster casual. Still gorgeous. Still intimidating.

She wished she had her boots on. Even an extra inch would give her a much needed boost. Then she saw the serious-looking man in a suit seated at the table, with serious-looking papers spread out before him.

'Take a seat, Stella,' Eduardo instructed.

'I prefer to stand,' she answered, glancing to where the Prince had paused at two seats on the opposite side of the table from the suited dude. She wasn't letting him dictate her every move. 'Always.'

'Okay,' he agreed, but something kindled in his eyes. 'But it is important that you pay attention to what Matteo tells you.'

'Why? You think I can't read all that for myself?' she asked softly, gesturing at the paperwork.

Despite that emotion still flickering, he chuckled and reached out, slowly brushing the tip of his finger over her lips in a sensual action. Stunned, she sucked in a breath and froze at the same time. His touch was gentle, yet firm, and not enough. He dropped his hand. She closed her mouth, holding back her bereft moan. She wanted the erotic sweep of his tongue. Memory surged, scorching her skin. He made her so hot all over.

His hand pressed on her shoulder and somehow she was sitting, weak-kneed, in the damn chair. Through dazed eyes she stared as he looked down at her with that gorgeous smile. Slowly the calculated alertness in his eyes dawned on her.

She glanced at the suit man and saw his amusement. He *knew* she couldn't resist Eduardo. Just like all his other women. That touch had been for show.

'Matteo and I were at law school together,' Eduardo explained smoothly, turning the papers around so they were in front of Stella. 'I am sure you will find everything clear, but if you don't he will answer any questions you may have.'

Eduardo had gone to law school?

'Are you paying attention, Stella?' He smiled at her.

She made herself stop staring at him and stared at the paperwork instead. The document wasn't long, and it wasn't written in convoluted legal speak either. It was all very, *very* clear. For every year they were married she would be awarded over a million dollars.

Her eyes widened when she saw the size of the settlement should their marriage end. And the stringent conditions attached to every payment.

'I'm never to speak to the media—or indeed anyone—about the details of our marriage?' she said. Did he seriously think she would?

'Nor am I,' he replied calmly.

But there weren't *penalties* for him should he do that. The money was already his. Hers only if she played by the rules he'd spelt out so clearly here.

He was trying to *buy* her. To control her.

The fire in her belly wasn't fuelled by desire now. It was all anger.

'I could never accept that much money from you,' she said quietly, her nose wrinkling in distaste at the divorce payout details.

'We're staying married, so you won't have to,' he soothed, but his gaze sharpened.

'It says here that if we have any children and we divorce, then the children must remain at the palace on San Felipe.' Her throat tightened as she paraphrased the passage.

This child would be *his*. He'd never allow her to have custody should she want to leave. He would control everything— for the duration of their sham marriage and beyond.

'It also says that you would be entitled to an apartment within the palace until any children we have reach the age of majority,' he nodded.

So if they divorced not long after their insane marriage— as was most likely—she would have to remain under his roof and watch him with a succession of lovers. A new wife, even.

That idea hurt more than it should.

'You cannot leave before then.' He misread the reason for her frown. 'I do not believe in depriving a child of its mother. But any child of mine will need to be educated within San Felipe. And my child will grow up at the palace.'

'What about your brother?' she asked. 'What if *he* marries and has children?'

Eduardo's expression was shuttered. 'Regardless of my brother's possible future family, there will always be a place for my children at the palace.'

'What if you marry again?' she whispered, understanding that he didn't really want to have this conversation in front of Matteo, but that it needed to be had.

'That is not going to happen. This is only to cover all eventualities.' He put his hand on her shoulder and his eyes were brilliant blue. He was angry with her for asking these questions. 'The truth is I will never let you go. And you know it.'

He slid his hand to the nape of her neck, bent and kissed her. It was a lie for his lawyer friend. But it was a beguiling, passionate lie. His mouth worked to subdue, to tempt, to make her open up and take what he offered.

And she couldn't resist. Her lips parted and his wicked tongue stroked deep. She almost moaned. But at the moment of surrender he drew back and looked down at her, his eyes hooded, his jaw set.

'Sign the document, Stella,' he said bluntly, his voice rising in volume.

The fire in his eyes was anger at her questions, not desire or jealousy or possessiveness. But all three of those things *she* felt. And the worst thing was that she was turned on—by the kiss, by the demand.

So stupid.

'Sign it so we can get back to better things,' he added.

The blatantly sensual implication stole her breath. Heat burned her cheeks when she saw him turn to glance arrogantly at Matteo.

Claiming territorial rights, much?

She straightened in her seat, pulling the neatly typed document closer. It was all very well planned, so nothing could be left in any doubt.

'Ms Zambrano...' Matteo spoke formally. 'I know prenuptial contracts can seem discomfiting, but I'm here more as your representative than the Prince's. He is well qualified to safeguard his own interests. So please be assured that this is a very generous offer.'

He was Eduardo's friend; they'd been law students together, so he was on Eduardo's side. And she didn't want any kind of 'generous offer'. She didn't want a wedding. She didn't want to go into this knowing they were going to *fail*. Here they were preparing for that very eventuality. But she didn't know what it was she did want.

The impossible? The fairy tale? Such things never happened in real life.

Eduardo was trying to protect their future. Reluctantly

she appreciated his integrity, but it irritated her at the same time that he could be so coolly rational about this nightmare. Clearly he wasn't thrown by their sexual chemistry the way she was.

It might be ungrateful, but something in her made her want to fight. A lifetime of training, she supposed. But if she tried to argue some more in front of the lawyer Eduardo would only get angrier and more determined. It might be better to sign now and fight when they were alone.

She picked up the gleaming fountain pen and made a scratchy mess of her signature.

'May I offer my congratulations?' Matteo gathered up the documents and put them into his briefcase.

'You may offer your hasty departure, my friend.' Eduardo escorted Matteo to the door. 'And your absolute discretion.'

'You don't need to tell me again.' Matteo turned and offered a small bow to Stella. 'It was an honour to meet you, Ms Zambrano.'

The ease of Eduardo's falsity alarmed her. Was he so well practised at presenting a façade and lying, even to his friends?

Restlessly she stood and walked the length of a bookcase, vaguely noticing the piles of personal papers and small ornaments tucked into the recesses amongst the leather-bound masterpieces.

'You don't trust me,' she said when the door had closed. Did he honestly think she would betray him?

'I don't know you,' Eduardo answered lightly, walking back towards her.

'Then get to know me.' She would *never* sell her story to the press. She was loyal to the core and deeply private.

'I intend to.' He smiled that wolfish smile. 'Intimately.'

Of course he'd reduce this to sex. Sex was so easy for him. *She'd* been so easy for him. Too late she realised the ramifications weren't as easy for her to handle.

'Do I get to do the same?' she questioned. 'Do I get to know you *beyond* "intimately"?'

His withdrawal was palpable. The easygoing façade fell in a blink, revealing a tense distance. And it wasn't just the smile that he dropped, but the warmth. That ruthlessness was exposed once more, making her realise just what a stranger to her he was.

'Of course.'

She ran her fingers over a smooth jet-black glass sculpture that stood on a low table. 'So you studied law?'

'For a couple of years, yes.' He turned away from her, choosing to sit at the table.

'Contracts and business and wheeling and dealing?' Like his sharp-suited friend?

'I preferred evidence—criminal law.' Another bare minimum answer.

'You wanted to be a courtroom lawyer?'

'It is impossible for me to work as a lawyer.'

'But you wanted to be one?' she pressed, curious about this side of him.

'We all want things we can't have.'

'Not princes.'

He hesitated, then cast a theatrical, mournful look at her. 'Especially princes.'

He'd slipped back into that 'Prince Eduardo' character—all roguish charm.

'I'm not about to feel sorry for you,' she said.

'Good. You're not marrying me out of pity, then.'

'I'm not marrying you for your money either,' she said, deadly serious.

'You can give it all away if you like.' He shrugged carelessly. 'Return to your room now. You have more preparations to attend to.'

'Seriously?' He was dismissing her? Just like that?

'Yes.' He looked unapologetic. 'Things to do, Stella.'

'Of course—your princely time is so precious.'

Stella walked back to her room, all senses on alert when she found her door was open. An older woman waited in the centre of the room alongside a wardrobe rack on wheels—the kind models had on fashion shoots.

'Miss Zambrano?'

'Yes.' Stella just stopped and stared.

'My name is Giulia. I'm here to help you dress tomorrow.'

Dress? Eduardo had been serious about her choosing a wedding dress? Given that the clothes rail was filled with dresses, it seemed he had.

'They are yours to try on. Choose your favourite and I will alter it as necessary.' The woman bent her head and smiled shyly. 'Any would look good on you.'

'Where did these come from?' Stella gazed along the rail, too scared to touch even though each creation was wrapped in protective plastic.

Seven dresses. All different styles. All obviously expensive.

'They were flown in from Paris and Milan.'

Stella read each carefully pinned label. High-fashion houses every one of them. Italian. French. American.

She'd never been a dress-up girl. Except for that one time she'd dressed up in her father's uniform. His fury had made her all the more determined to earn one of her own—to be better than the son he'd wanted and never got. Only her father had sent her away to school on the other side of the world. Out of sight, out of mind.

'Allow me to show you each dress.' Giulia suddenly took charge. 'I realise it can be difficult to make a decision when they are all so exquisite.'

Enraptured by the yards of silk, satin and lace, Giulia took a good twenty minutes showing and explaining the unique features of each.

'Have you worked for Eduardo long?' Stella asked when the servant had hung the last dress back on the rack.

Giulia's eyes clouded and she retreated back behind her quiet reserve. 'A number of years.'

'I bet you didn't think he'd ever marry.' Stella tried to

smile, as if joking. 'He's "the untameable prince", right?' She used the media's favourite description of him.

'It has long been expected that Eduardo will marry. Both he and Antonio deserve happy marriages.' Giulia stood haughtily.

'Which do you think *he'd* like?' Stella stopped trying to smile and stared at the dresses. It wasn't that she wanted to please him, but it was clear that Giulia did.

Giulia glanced briefly at Stella, then moved to the last dress she'd held up. A tumble of soft, pretty silk with embroidered flowers trailing down the edges. The flowers gave just a trace of colour to the dress and reminded her of spring.

Stella held up her hands and shook her head. 'It's too fussy, with all that detail.'

'It is modest, yet modern. You should try it.'

Well, she had to start somewhere. Self-consciously Stella stripped to her underwear and stepped into the beautiful dress, holding still so Giulia could fasten it.

Five minutes later she stared at herself in the mirror, trying not to let her shock show on her face. It wasn't as if she hadn't worn a dress before—she just didn't do it that often—and this dress...

'You're sure it's okay?' She swung to face Giulia.

'Are you comfortable in it?' Undeniably smug, Giulia was smiling.

'Yes.' Stella realised she was more than comfortable. Who knew that putting on a dress could make her feel different? Brave. Beautiful. It was like a costume in which she'd play a part. Or a uniform. *Armour.*

'Then it is the one.' Giulia made small adjustments to the waist and the hem and pinned them.

'That was easy.'

'When you know, you know. It is the same when choosing a groom, *si*?' Giulia suddenly chuckled softly. 'I will bring you a dinner tray now. Then you should rest. You have a big day tomorrow.'

Stella paused. 'I'm not dining with Eduardo?'

'He has business to attend to.'

The little pleasure Stella had felt at discovering the dress disappeared. Now, left alone in the room with the other possible wedding dresses, the full horror of it sank into her bones.

Any dress would have done, right? As would any bride. Rumour had it the upcoming autumn ball was to have been a 'find a bride' event in disguise, for the pair of princes. Eduardo didn't want to marry, but was 'expected' to. In other words, at some point he *had* to. And look what fate had so conveniently provided. A pregnant lover.

Not desired. Not loved. Merely convenient.

Stella rubbed her chilled arms. Could she really go through with this mockery? Even if it was only temporary? Or did she not want to *because* it was only temporary?

Her heart skipped faster as her thoughts veered too close to the uncomfortable. She knew her parents had loved each other. She'd seen it in the pictures her father had hidden away because they hurt him too much. He'd withdrawn into his work.

At the thought of her mother, fear unfurled.

Impatiently she walked over to the fresh tray that had been delivered to her room. She forced herself to eat, even though she couldn't be less hungry. Not because Eduardo had told her to, but because the child within her needed sustenance. Stella had to stay strong and healthy. She couldn't let her child down. She couldn't make her mum's mistake.

She ate quickly, quietly, alone. How many times in her life had she eaten with no one to talk to? No companionship. No support. Just a few bites of food—fuel and nothing more.

He has business to attend to.

Was her future to be an echo of her past? Would they share carefully scheduled meetings at mealtimes in which they'd swap shallow pleasantries and stilted conversation?

It would be just like the relationship she had with her father. Work had always come first for him. Clearly it was the same for Eduardo. Fair enough. He was a prince with bigger things to worry about than her fragile ego.

But this was no longer only about her. She didn't want her child to suffer the way she had.

She forced a few more mouthfuls down and then gave up on the effort. She'd finally realised the full import of this crazy day.

What was best for this baby wasn't what Eduardo thought. He meant well, but marriage wasn't necessary. No one ever need know it was *his* baby. She could rear the child in private and they could all be free to be happy.

Resolve firming, she left her room and swiftly walked along the sumptuous corridors back to the library. It was empty, but in the distance she heard a regular splashing sound.

Business to attend to, huh?

She went out through one of the French doors to the terrace and walked the length of the building, then turned the corner to find a private lap pool. She crept closer, pausing beside a tall column. Wicker chairs covered in plump, pure white cushions sat at angles to each other, but she didn't take a seat. She couldn't take her eyes from the strong figure gliding smoothly through the aquamarine water. She watched him complete several lengths, executing perfect tumble turns at each end, easily maintaining that scorching pace.

But halfway through the next length he suddenly stopped and stood. Droplets of water cascaded down his broad shoulders. 'How long are you going to stand in the shadows watching me?'

He had good eyesight, then. So did she. And right now he looked incredibly athletic. Fit, strong, *built*.

'I want to talk to you,' she said, glad that dusk was darkening the sky and half-hiding the blush she knew was covering every inch of her body.

He levered himself out of the pool in one smooth movement and stood before her. 'So talk.'

Her jaw dropped. 'You're…naked.' And she was no longer blushing—she was *burning*.

'It is my pool.' He shrugged. 'My staff know not to bother me.'

'I'm not staff.' That was precisely the point she needed to make. She wasn't going to be ordered about and dismissed. She'd damn well bother him when she wanted to.

He inclined his head. 'I was not expecting company.'

'You want to make yourself decent?' Desperately she glanced around for a towel, to stop herself staring at him like a lust-struck, hormone-drunk wanton.

'Am I not already?' He sent her an ironic glance. 'You were naked before and not embarrassed. I'm not embarrassed by you seeing me. In fact, I quite like it.'

CHAPTER SIX

EDUARDO WAS TEASING the tiger. He shouldn't. He was too close to losing control. But he couldn't resist.

He wasn't going to like what she'd come to say. He could read it in her diamond-bright eyes and firm-held mouth. On the plus side, he relished the fact that his nudity had shot her concentration. That made them even.

He didn't want to fight. He was mentally worn out from the day's revelations and resulting requirements, and he absolutely shouldn't have kissed her before because it was all he could think about now.

He'd spent hours organising every damn detail and all he wanted now was for the next few to pass quickly so he could complete his plan. Then he could have her—how he wanted, where he wanted. All would work out. It had to.

'You really are the most arrogant pri—' she growled in a low, rusty voice.

'Arrogant prince—yes.' He readily admitted it. 'We're born that way.' He reached past her for a towel, letting his hand brush her denim-clad thigh. 'Now, tell me the problem—cold feet?'

'I'm not marrying you tomorrow.'

He wrapped the towel round his waist and then just looked at her.

She stared back, obviously waiting for a reply, but he'd learned a few tricks from his ice-cold brother. When the silence grew too much for her to bear—as he had known it would—she started talking.

'It's a bad idea. You know it's not necessary.'

He remained unmoved.

'I can go away and take care of the baby. We don't need to do this.'

She was so wrong.

'You don't need me?' Anger clouded his vision. 'What can you give this child alone?' he asked, determined to remain calm. 'You would travel to some distant place, put the child in daycare for all hours while you work to feed and shelter it?'

'How is that worse than an army of nannies and a distant father the child will see for five minutes a day if it's lucky?'

'Why assume I'll be a distant father?'

Her eyes flashed with disbelief.

His anger roiled at her rejection. Why did she judge him so harshly? She had no reason to, and yet she hadn't given him a chance. Not once. Right from the beginning she'd kept the most important things from him. She hadn't told him her name, hadn't told him she was a virgin. She'd used him, then left him hanging. And then she hadn't even told him she was expecting. Instead she'd tried to flee. Did she think that little of him?

'You would deny your child's birthright?'

'*You* would ensure he or she missed out on nothing.' Anger flushed her cheeks.

'So...' He nodded bitterly. 'You only want cash from me.'

'This isn't about me or what I want.' She glared at him.

'The hell it isn't.' It damn well *was* about her. And him. And this insane pull they shared. She didn't like it. Well, nor did he. But they were both going to have to get over it. This time he was getting it right.

'This is about what's best for our baby. Think about it.' She switched to a calm tone that made him suspicious. 'Together we can arrange for this child to have a quiet, happy life out of the spotlight. He or she wouldn't suffer the burden of royal expectation or protocol. No duty to fulfil. No desire to be denied.'

Oh, she was smart—picking up on the smallest hint of discomfort within him and using it to bolster her argument. The fact that she was so astute invigorated him. But that she could so easily dismiss the idea that he might have anything more than money to offer *burned*.

'But it could never be kept secret. Would you be happy to play the role of unmarried mother?' he growled back, his temper slipping his hold because her words had struck hard. 'Of fallen woman?'

'This is the twenty-first century—children are born out of wedlock all the time. Kids grow up in sole-parent households all over the world—'

'Not in the De Santis family,' he interrupted harshly. 'Honour above all else.' He captured her hand in a hard grip and pulled her closer. He clamped his other arm around her. It felt damn good to touch her—even if she was spitting fire.

'Honour?' she snarled. 'You call this sham wedding honourable? It is deceit.'

'There is no deceit,' he argued hotly. 'We will be married for real. What is it that you want from me?' he exploded, pushing her away from him so he could think. 'I am doing what's right. I am being reasonable. You want me to tie you up in chains and drag you to the altar? Would that make you feel better in some warped way? You want me to play lord and master?'

But Stella didn't walk away as he'd expected her to. No, she stepped right back into his personal space.

'*Play?* You *are* dragging me to the altar.'

'You do not want this marriage. Fine. Nor do I. But we must do what is right and best for the baby, for the royal family—an institution far bigger and more important than us two individuals. That is the reality. Accept it. Be the mother you want to be *here*, in San Felipe.' He stopped and dragged in a breath, frustrated as hell. 'And when we are alone I will not take that which you do not want to give. That which you do not want.'

She tempted him to the point of madness, but he was more of a man than that.

'I know you wouldn't.'

She took the wind out of his sails. For a half-second he just stared. But a need for more of her honesty burned through any reticence he had left.

'But you want me. Don't try to deny it.' He spoke through

clenched teeth. 'Don't lie to me.' There was nothing he hated more than that.

'I didn't.' Stormily she glared back up at him. 'I won't.'

The sulky, sultry words tore through the last of his control. He put his hand on her back and pulled her close until she was pressed tightly against him. 'So, in your version of the future, what would you see us doing about *this*?'

There was no hiding his desire, and hers was equally obvious. She might have put her hands on his chest to hold him at a small distance, but her fingers spread and stroked, as if she couldn't resist touching what she could of him. Her body shivered on impact against his, before softening to accommodate and mould to him. Her erect nipples were beautiful beacons, calling for his attention; so was her reddened, pouting mouth.

But she hesitated before answering. 'There's no reason why we can't indulge for a while.'

She licked her lips, but despite the cool breathiness with which she spoke there was no hiding the hint of anxiety in her huge eyes.

He ought to laugh. Instead he was infuriated.

She would try to act the coquette? This woman had avoided physical pleasure for so long and now she was acting as if she was hard enough to cope with *that* game? Did she intend to acquiesce to a series of meaningless temporary affairs after screwing around with him for a while?

He would never treat her as a disposable sex partner who'd happened to get pregnant. Never let anyone else. The playgirls of minor princes in Europe were often passed from one wealthy lover to the next like possessions—the toys *du jour*. It wasn't a scene he had any part of, for all his carefree reputation. The thought of any of those men laying a finger on her scalded his flesh.

Nor would he let the press hound her. Already they reported endlessly on any possible affair of his. Her private life would be up for public speculation, gossip and innuendo. Without palace protection—and control—she might succumb to the need to feed the machine. She might be tempted to sell her story.

Never happening.

She needed the protection of his ring. So did the child. And he would ensure they had it, so that when this ended she would have the dignity and respect of having been his *wife*. She would have honour, a permanent position. He would ensure the blame for the break-up would be his burden alone.

And she'd admitted her attraction to him. Satisfaction scoured his anger. Rampant sexual anticipation reared. He ached for her surrender to his kiss, to his wishes, to her own pleasure.

Rough desire drew him to mutter in her ear. 'Your body has known no other but mine. Your body craves mine. And the baby it carries is mine,' he said rawly, his reason lost. '*You* are mine.'

'I am not a thing to be owned...' A shaken whisper, and then her face lifted—unbearably, kissably close to his.

'No, you are a woman to be treasured. Respected.'

'I am a *soldier*,' she corrected through gritted teeth.

'You are determined to fight?' Adrenalin primed his muscles. A bed was the best battleground for them.

'I'm not that immature. But it is my job to protect. Defend.'

'What is it that's so in need of protection? What defence is required when you know I only want what's best for this baby? When you know I will move heaven and earth to ensure it is safe? Perhaps it is not the child you are protecting. Perhaps it is yourself.'

Her vividly blue eyes widened. 'I'm not afraid of you.'

'No? Are you not a little afraid of *this*?' He slid his hand over the curve of her butt and around her beautiful long thighs, slipped his fingers up in between them. Even through the old denim he could feel the heat of her. 'Is that what all this bluster is about? You said yes to me, but was it too intense that day on the beach? Did sweet, virginal Stella get more than she bargained for?' Ordinarily he'd offer a smile with this teasing, but he was too hard, too serious, because he feared this was the truth. 'Is that why you ran away?'

Her beautiful mouth parted. Her shadowed eyes locked on his. 'I'd had what I wanted,' she said. '*All* that I wanted. So I left.'

'All you wanted?' He shook his head. He really didn't think so. Not when he could feel her so tense with need in his arms now.

'Sex has consequences,' she whispered.

'Not just physical,' he agreed softly. 'Not just the baby.' He sighed. 'You were very inexperienced.'

Hot emotion flashed in her eyes. 'That doesn't make me an idiot. Or a coward.' She tossed her head and inched her feet apart, inviting him to stroke her even more intimately. 'Take me now and see how scared I am.'

The thin threads of his self-control started to snap.

He'd swum length after length to take the edge off the desire that had dominated him since he'd clapped eyes on her again. Maybe he shouldn't have left her alone. Maybe she needed something else.

He skimmed his fingers higher, stroked harder. He smiled, almost purring at her sigh, at the rotation of her hips that gave her away completely.

'If I were to kiss you there now—' his voice roughened '—I think I would find you wetter than you were in that shower.'

He was pushing too close to his own limits. To hers. But he couldn't resist. He had to touch her. He'd give anything for a taste. He watched her through hooded lids, seeing her lips part in invitation, hearing her breathing quicken to match her small movements as he stroked her.

'Don't...' she said brokenly. 'Stop.'

Eduardo momentarily closed his eyes, breathing in her delicate scent as her words echoed in his head. Just two words, yet their meaning could be read in two—polar opposite—ways. He had to err on the side of caution.

So he stopped.

Her groan—and the look of pure chagrin in her eyes—told him he'd made the wrong choice. But it was the right one for now.

'Poor Stella.' He put his hands on her shoulders for a second, to ensure she had her balance. 'It has been a tough day.'

She gasped. 'I hate you.'

He half laughed. That comeback was so weak, and it told him so much he was unable to resist rubbing his hand down her back again. So lithe and warm and willing, and everything he wanted. 'Hate away. You still want me.'

He was dying of want for her.

'You're going to hate being married to me.' Her breathing hitched again.

But he was going to love giving her a wedding night she'd never forget.

By signing those confidentiality clauses and the prenup contract she'd acquiesced to the control he needed. He'd reward her. He'd indulge every sensual fantasy with her like this—moving and moaning, her body hot, her eyes hungry. So hungry she hurt. He'd help her understand the pleasure of this kind of passion and then it could burn itself out within the safety of their marriage. Ultimately their child would be cared for. Their futures would be assured.

His plan was perfect.

'You will have me,' he promised huskily, drawing on all his self-control so he was able to step back. 'Once we are married.'

Stella stifled another embarrassing moan of disappointment as Eduardo gently pulled his hand away from the small of her back. Her heart beat wildly…her body felt jumpy. So easily he had seduced her into agreeing—again. So easily he had won. So easily he could have her stupidly weak body.

'But not before then, Stella.'

He knew how much she wanted his touch, knew he could wield the power of it over her. That he could control his own desire for her was alarming. He totally had the upper hand.

All the fight fell from her. All that was left was an unbearably empty ache. She might almost cry. But Stella never cried.

'I'm going to bed,' she mumbled.

'Not yet.'

She shook her head. 'You can't keep ordering me around. I won't do what you say. I'm not your servant. Not your soldier. I'm Stella. Your equal.'

He stepped back and held out his hand, that roguish smile curving his lips. 'Please.'

Eduardo the 'Fun in San Felipe' poster boy was back. Charming, slightly wicked, irresistible.

Finally she realised. He used it to get his own way—knew he could seduce her into saying yes to anything. So perhaps the best strategy was for her to let him *think* he was getting his way and work on her resistance from inside the marriage. It was only a temporary thing anyway, wasn't it? Maybe if she played it right she'd be able to convince him to let her and the child live in some nice house on one of the smaller islands after they divorced. If she was agreeable now—

'Stella.'

She took his hand and he led her back along the terrace and then into the library. Her pulse skipped again at that simplest of touches. While she was relieved he'd wrapped the towel around his waist, it sat too snug and low on his hips, revealing his rock-hard, ridged abs. She forced her eyes front.

A sleek black case was on the desk. Eduardo pressed his thumb on the edge of it and Stella heard electronic beeping, then the unmistakable sounds of locks sliding open.

'How very spy movie,' Stella muttered.

But when he lifted the lid and pulled away the black velvet cloth covering the contents she couldn't hold back her gasp.

Jewels. Necklaces. Tiaras. Rings.

'No.' She blinked rapidly, her decision to be agreeable zapped by the gleaming brilliance of so many precious stones and the subtle meaning they represented.

Eduardo was looking at her with a quizzical expression. 'My bride must wear—'

'I can't wear any of these,' she interrupted. She never wore jewellery. She didn't even have her ears pierced. She didn't fancy having it used against her in combat. 'What do you do? Keep a selection on hand for all your mistresses?'

He sent her a sideways look. 'I don't have mistresses.'

'Not while we are married,' she snapped back.

'You think you need to tell me that?' He actually laughed.

'You had sex with me within ten seconds of talking to me,' she reminded him.

'And *you* had sex with *me* within ten seconds of talking to me. So the same rule applies to you,' he answered mildly. 'I already know I am going to have to work extremely hard to keep you sated.'

Bereft of words, she could only glare at him. He turned away, his lips twitching.

'These are not trinkets tossed to temporary lovers to placate them,' he explained quietly. 'These are royal jewels. Gifts from centuries past, kept within the family vaults and treasured for their personal value as much as for their supposed price. Which will you wear tomorrow?'

'None.' She couldn't possibly pick any of them. She didn't want to be adorned, to be reduced to a decoration. That hadn't ever been a role of her choosing.

'You do not even want to see them?' A hint of steel underpinned the question.

'No. I don't wear jewellery.' If she did she'd feel even more like a fake.

'If you will not choose I will choose for you.'

'They're all amazing,' she said, trying to pull together some politeness. 'But I don't want to wear any of them.'

'My bride will wear what is appropriate and what is expected.' She felt his gaze hard on her. 'I will send my selection to you in the morning. If you are not wearing them I'll put them on you myself.'

It was a threat. A promise.

'Why do you want me all dolled up?' she asked, not understanding him at all. 'What's the point? This is an elopement, right? No one is going to see me anyway.'

'*I* am going to see you.'

That edge in his voice sliced, letting the lust within her stream out. Like smoke in a jar it swirled, constantly seeking escape—*release*.

'I'm going to see *all* of you,' he promised.

She knew he wanted to see only her body. He wasn't interested in her soul.

And wasn't that okay? She wasn't interested in his either. She refused to be.

'Then fine—whatever you want.' She stepped back. 'Send it to my room and I will wear it.'

'So you are not going to jilt me?' His lips twitched again, but there was seriousness in his eyes.

'I'll be there,' she replied.

What choice did she have? She would marry Eduardo because he was right. He could give this child so much that she couldn't. Together, they would give this child the best chance possible.

She'd stay fit. She'd survive the birth. And she'd tell her baby every single day how much she loved it. History was not repeating itself.

She'd marry a man who didn't love her. She'd make that sacrifice because already she loved her baby. And she would do whatever was necessary to protect and defend not just its physical safety, but its emotional safety too. She'd give her baby everything she hadn't had.

But at the same time she had to keep her heart safe. She had to rid herself of this physical infatuation as quickly as she could.

She walked out of the room without glancing back at him. 'See you at the altar, Eduardo.'

CHAPTER SEVEN

AT FIVE-THIRTY THE next morning Stella rose and laced up her trainers. Despite almost zero sleep, she was so full of energy she needed to burn it off—hard and fast. She saw no one as she ran the gravel track looping the small island, but she knew her action wasn't unseen.

Sure enough, when she got back Eduardo was waiting at the top of the stone stairs, looking annoyingly cool in black trousers and a white shirt.

'Isn't it bad luck to see me before the ceremony?' she asked, as breathless as if she'd run round the track ten times, not two.

'The new day has scarcely started. I do not think this counts.' He looked down at her, his expression unreadable. 'What are you doing?'

'What does it look like I'm doing?' she mocked. 'Did you think I was trying to run away? I have many talents, but walking on water isn't one of them.'

'After your reckless rock-climbing escape that day at Cala de Piratas, I wouldn't put it past you to try and swim to the mainland.'

'I know about the rip between those two islands.'

'But you like to take risks more than you're willing to admit?' he countered, his expression amused.

'Not stupid ones. I know my own strength.'

'And you must also know that my security detail is watching every centimetre of this island's perimeter. No one arrives. Or leaves.'

'That's a threat?'

'No, that's just the way it is.' He shrugged.

'Always?' Were his moments always so closely monitored? Even when he was on 'holiday'?

'Yes.' His frown deepened as he watched her struggle to regulate her breathing. 'It can't be healthy for the baby for you to be working out to such an extreme level.'

'This isn't extreme.' She stiffened defensively. 'Get your doctor back if you don't believe me.' She needed to see that doctor again, to talk through her history properly. *Privately.*

'I will. You might not obey orders from me, but you will listen to him. Agreed?'

'Of course.' She climbed to the top of the stairs and stood directly in front of him, but he didn't move to let her pass.

He brushed the side of her face with the back of his fingers. 'Did you sleep at all?'

The bed had been enormous, clad in luxury linen, soft and decadent—nothing like the narrow, hard beds at the barracks. It hadn't been built for one person to sleep in.

'I can't think why I didn't,' she answered acerbically, fighting the way she was drawn to him. 'Maybe it was the life-changing revelations of yesterday that had me all antsy.'

'Maybe,' he murmured. 'But maybe it was something else altogether.'

She glared up at him, provoked. 'You think you're irresistible?'

'Past form would indicate that you like what I do to you.' He was charming again. Impulsive. Teasing. But he didn't touch her again. Instead he glanced at the platinum watch on his wrist. 'You had better run now—so you can get ready for our wedding.'

'I'm not the kind of woman who takes two hours to get dressed.' She folded her arms and sent him a surly look. 'Why *is* the ceremony so early?'

'So our wedding night can last as long as possible.' He laughed wickedly. 'Why did you think?'

'You're impossible.' And alarmingly irresistible.

'Actually, I think you'll find I'm very easy to please.' He nodded over her shoulder and she turned to see that the sea and sky were painted rose-gold as the sun started its slow ascent. 'It's a beautiful day to get married,' he said softly.

It *was* a beautiful day. Yet suddenly she was terrified. She was out of her depth.

'Say yes.' That brightness in his eyes hardened.

He *knew*. He'd said it last night…more than he'd bargained for. Not the baby, but the maelstrom of emotion he aroused in her. Even now lust curled through her unruly body, tightening her muscles with anticipation.

'I won't obey your every dictate.' Somehow she needed to keep this desire within her control.

His smile lit up.

'That wasn't a challenge,' she added, far too late. Flames of anticipation licked.

'We both know it was.' But he stepped back and turned towards the palace. 'I'll see you when the sun has fully risen.'

When she got to her room Giulia was waiting there, beautifully dressed in a soft blue suit.

'You're back,' she said crisply. 'I have the dress finished and pressed. And Prince Eduardo has sent this.'

Stella walked towards the velvet envelope Giulia had placed on the dresser. Pulse skidding, she opened it and drew a soft breath. It wasn't the blinding, million diamonds showpiece she'd expected. This was a huge single sapphire pendant, simply set on a beautiful platinum twist. There was stunning fire in its depths.

'Oh…'

Stella turned at the whisper. Giulia was staring at the stone. 'You know it?' Stella asked.

'Midnight's Passion.' Giulia nodded. 'One of the most famous in the royal collection. It has a very romantic history attached to it.' Giulia glanced at her speculatively. 'Perfect for an elopement.'

This didn't seem like much of an elopement when he had everything planned to perfection—palace, dress, make-up, jewellery, prenup.

'You must get ready,' Giulia reminded her quietly.

An hour later Stella stood still while Giulia finished smoothing her dress and assessed her.

'*Si.*' She nodded. 'You look nice.'

Part of Stella had been hoping for a little more than 'nice', but then she had refused Giulia's offer of a manicure. He'd have to take her as she was. She wasn't going to change for him. This wedding was only about the baby.

But Giulia had a sly look in her eye. 'I will do your hair.' She took the brush before Stella could reply.

'You refused a tiara?'

'It didn't seem right.' Stella sat in the chair Giulia had set for her.

'Of course.' Giulia nodded. 'I have something else.'

She had a selection of tiny tight rosebuds that mirrored the delicate detail on the edge of Stella's dress. With nimble fingers Giulia braided Stella's hair, weaving flowers into it and then leaving part of it loose at the back. Then she carefully settled the veil on her head.

'You must miss your mother today,' Giulia said softly.

'She died a long time ago.' Stella hardly ever let herself think about her. And she refused to now. She also refused to think of her father.

'You and the Prince have much in common,' Giulia said.

No, they really didn't.

Giulia placed a beautiful linen cloth over Stella's dress, then came towards her with a make-up brush. 'Close your eyes.'

'I don't usually wear much make-up,' Stella protested weakly.

'You don't need much.' Giulia nodded. 'I will only accentuate here and there.'

Instinctively Stella knew she could trust Giulia, and also knew that part of her wanted to surprise Eduardo. He probably expected that she'd stomp up the aisle wearing jeans and a frown. Maybe she could startle *him* into submission.

'You're smiling.' Giulia sounded pleased as she worked. 'It suits you.'

Ten minutes later Stella scarcely recognised herself in the

mirror. What had Giulia done to make her skin glow like that? And her eyes sparkle?

Giulia handed her a bouquet of roses. 'I gathered these from the garden this morning.'

Stella breathed in the delicate scent. 'They're beautiful. Thank you.'

'Wishing you health, fertility, happiness.'

A gleam in the older woman's eye made Stella suspect she knew the truth.

'Put your shoes on—he'll be waiting.'

'Where is he?' Stella asked as she followed Giulia outside and down a pathway through the intricate formal garden.

'The family chapel.'

They were having a *church* wedding? Somehow she'd imagined a quick service with a celebrant in that enormous library, or something.

She followed Giulia to the outer reaches of the magnificent garden. A small stone building was enveloped in greenery. Ancient but lovingly tended roses smothered the masonry, giving it an incredibly romantic look.

'Wait here a moment,' Giulia instructed. 'I will check that everything is ready.'

In other words she'd make sure Eduardo was there.

Stella lifted her bouquet again to breathe in the gorgeous aroma, smiling to herself at the ludicrous thought of the Prince being late—or, even better, getting cold feet and standing her up. But after a short moment Giulia appeared in the doorway and beckoned to her.

The trailing rose vines arched over the doorway, their beauty and perfume drawing her in. Stella stepped over the threshold and smiled sadly at the irony. It was the most beautiful wedding setting she could have imagined—roses and old stone, glimmering gold, flickering candles and velvet. And all for a loveless, temporary pretence.

But then she looked to the front of the chapel, just as Eduardo turned and looked at her, and that low ache in her heart simply dissolved.

Clad in full royal regalia, he stood tall and silent and solemn, looking absolutely like the 'handsome Prince' in a lush Hollywood adaptation of a traditional fairy tale—from the slightly long hair to the blue and gold sash across his chest, the highly polished boots to the gleaming ceremonial sword at his side.

The exquisitely decorated chapel faded from her view. All she could do was look, and all she could see was him. His gaze was unwavering. He watched as she hesitated, as she desperately drew a calming breath. Her whole body seemed to be alight with nerves and anticipation. Stupidly, she hoped her appearance pleased him the way his did her.

And then he smiled. It wasn't a smile she'd seen before—this one was sudden and infectious, and the slightest dimple appeared in his cheek.

It was so very unfair of him.

Emotion surged from some deep well within her—an overwhelming, driving need to move closer to him. Crazy as it was, nothing could have stopped her from putting one foot in front of the other. Nothing could have stopped her moving towards that deep, inscrutable promise she read in his eyes. Magnetic, irresistible, her attraction to him was overwhelming.

Vaguely she heard words, repeated them when necessary, watched almost as if from a distance as Giulia took the bouquet from her and Eduardo took her hand. She looked down as he loosely clasped her icy fingers in his.

Her nails were neatly clipped and unpolished. Unrefined. Like the rest of her. She was built for service, not decoration, and she'd always clearly delineated that aspect of herself. She wasn't going to be accused of being a 'dolly' soldier. But now she wished she'd said yes to Giulia's offer of a manicure.

She gazed at the thick platinum band he'd slid onto her finger. And he had another ring—a sapphire as deep and cloudy blue as the heavy stone resting in her décolletage. He placed the second ring on her finger, after the first. She knew they were for show, but still they felt significant.

Giulia said something and Stella turned. The woman gave her a thick, heavy band. It took a moment for her to realise it was for her to give to Eduardo. His nails, too, were neatly clipped and unpolished. For a foolish half-second she wished they could be suited as easily as that. She fumbled to get the ring onto his finger and he had to help. She heard him muttering something softly but couldn't look at him. Her emotions were too intense and he read them too easily.

He kept hold of her hands, warming them as the ceremony continued, and finally the priest uttered the fateful words.

They were now husband and wife. They could kiss.

Silence fell. She stared at the shining medals placed over his heart, unable to look higher. Then she realised he was waiting for her. Finally she summoned her courage and looked up into his face.

His eyes were burning so very blue, gleaming with the desire—the fiery impulsiveness—that had captured them both so completely that day on the beach.

She wanted to speak, to pull him back to reality. But it was too late. He bent his head and pressed his lips to hers. A fleeting whisper of a kiss.

Not enough. Not the demand she'd expected and wanted.

He looked into her eyes again, silently reading her reaction. All she could do was look back at him—she couldn't look away, couldn't hide now.

Then it came. And the spark of recognition engulfed them both.

He wrapped both arms tightly about her, pulling her almost off her feet. She clung to the fabric stretched over his chest, seeking a hold as passion swept her away with him once more. Opening up, she let him in, almost angrily giving him what he sought. What she needed too. Sensations rose from deep within...any last restraint was unleashed. She poured her anger, her uncertainty and her sheer raw need into her kiss. His arms tightened. So did hers. She needed to feel him like this—so powerful, so focused, all-encompassing.

But then he broke the divine contact—barely lifting his head, his embrace still fierce.

'Leave us,' he commanded thickly.

She trembled at the passion in his voice, at the look in his eyes—the raw *intent*.

'Sir, sorry...' Someone interrupted with an apologetic cough. 'You must sign... To make it official.'

Eduardo didn't move. Arousal and irritation and amusement and apology flickered in his eyes like a spinning kaleidoscope of beautiful bright colour. 'Official?' he echoed grimly.

Finally he loosened his grip on her. Stella glanced up and saw that Matteo, the lawyer, was there. She hadn't noticed him when she'd walked in. But of course—he was here to act as witness. And that was, in part, why Eduardo had kissed her so passionately. It had been for show. To make this *official*.

That was why they were here, after all.

Eduardo paused for another moment, ensuring that she was balanced, but she had her iron core back. Something flashed in his eyes as he rapidly stepped away and silently signed the thick parchment spread on an ornate wooden table to the side of the altar.

Stella followed, her hand shaking, leaving her name an illegible mess. Giulia and Matteo signed as their witnesses.

'Now leave us,' Eduardo ordered, curling his hand around Stella's wrist.

Her agitated pulse skipped and skidded against his fingers. Matteo threw his friend a broad smile and offered his arm to Giulia to escort her out. Giulia, Stella noted dazedly, was also smiling broadly. The pair followed the priest down the aisle and out of the building. Not one of them said anything more. Not one of them looked back.

Stella remained still, her knees locked, her emotions tumultuous. The intensity of her desire was out of control—and frankly it scared her.

He turned to her. His intention clear.

Another kiss and she'd lose her mind altogether, so searing was the heat that flared between them. Desperately she put her hand on his chest, stopping his progression towards her.

'We *can't*,' she said, scandalised. 'This is a church.'

'This is the family chapel,' he corrected huskily. 'The De Santis sanctuary for centuries.'

'Even more reason not to indulge in...' She trailed off, surprised to see his face light with laughter.

'What? Animal passions?' He laughed aloud then. 'These walls have seen worse. But come...' He held out his hand to her.

His first command as her husband. And what an innuendo.

He looked so happy, so pleased with himself—as if a huge burden had been lifted from his shoulders—and she was so surprised and seduced by that charming good humour that she'd placed her hand in his before she'd thought better of it.

He didn't turn to walk her back down the aisle. Rather he led her to a small wrought-iron gate, hidden beyond the altar. Through the railings she could see a curved stone staircase, going underground. He took a key from his pocket, unlocked the gate and led her through it.

She tugged on his hand just as he took the first step of the spiral down. He paused and looked at her. 'You're taking me to the *crypt*?' she asked, horrified.

'You really do think I'm charming, don't you?' he said blandly. 'First the chapel, and now you think I intend to desecrate the dead with lewd acts?' He shook his head, and suddenly that laughing sparkle in his eyes was snuffed out. The ruthless solemnity returned and he spoke very quietly. 'You must think you've married a monster.'

She couldn't look at his expression, her body shrinking in shame at the tinge of hurt she'd heard. 'I don't really *know* the man I've married.' And she didn't know how to handle the feelings he aroused in her.

'You could try to trust me, just a very little.' He watched her intently. 'I've given you no reason *not* to trust me.'

That was true. He was only trying to do what he thought was the right thing. As was she. But she didn't trust easily.

'Okay,' she said softly. 'I'll try.' She curled her fingers around his. 'You know…' She offered a tentative, peace-making smile. 'If this whole prince thing doesn't work out for you, you could do really well as a wedding planner.'

He looked startled for a second, and then his laugh returned. An answering spurt of pleasure bubbled up within her.

'Is that a compliment?' He shook his head. 'Undeserved, sadly. I have very good aides.'

Maybe, but he'd been the one to order it all.

'Where does this lead, if not the crypt?' she asked as they went further down the old narrow steps.

'There is a safe escape. The pirates' secret, as you've so often suggested.'

'Seriously?'

'Absolutely.' The laughter burned in his eyes once more. So did the desire. 'I'm dragging you to my pirate lair and I am going to have my wicked way with you.'

'And you expect me to trust you?' she teased, excitement fluttering low in her belly.

'You can trust that it'll be *very* wicked.'

At the bottom of the stairs there was a marble-lined tunnel. He hadn't been joking about the passageway.

There were gas lanterns every eight feet, giving off a flickering romantic light. They turned a narrow corner and the tunnel opened into a small cavern. In the centre stood a massive bed decked with lush linen—white sheets, heaps of plump pillows, a charcoal-black mohair blanket folded into a neat square. More lanterns hung in each corner. Beyond the bed faint light flickered in one corner of the gloom—the tunnel must continue.

It was totally over the top, but so magnificent.

Having taken several moments to absorb the opulence, she turned to him. 'You never do anything by halves, do you?'

'I like to do things as well as I can. To do my best.' He smiled.

He wasn't talking decor any more. The trouble was, his 'best' overwhelmed her and her own response terrified her. To have given him her virginity so quickly and easily—without so much as a second thought—that day on the beach...

Eduardo lifted his hand and gently framed her face. 'Not in a rush.'

She knew he'd felt her tremble.

'Not this time,' he promised.

CHAPTER EIGHT

'GIULIA SAID THIS sapphire is called Midnight's Passion.'
Stella drew in a jagged breath. 'Why did you choose it?'

Something shadowed his face. The smile on his lips
twisted. 'It matches the colour of the sea and the sky on the
day we met. I look at it and I see you. It suits you.'

No one had given her jewellery. Ever. She didn't know
what her father had done with her mother's things—he never
discussed her.

Eduardo watched her. 'It brings out that blue in your eyes
and you look even more beautiful. Which is impossible, but
there it is.'

For a half-second she stared at him, then turned away.

He grasped her arm and turned her back to him. 'You're
not used to receiving compliments?'

Her tongue was tied. She didn't want to answer that honestly. She didn't want pity.

'When someone compliments you, you say thank you. It
is very simple. But failing that—' his boyish dimpled grin
exploded '—you let actions speak.' He held up a hand in defence. 'Just a smile. I didn't mean sex. Though of course I
would not say no to that.'

She laughed. As he'd intended her to.

'You will learn you can trust me,' he said softly.

'And will you trust *me*?' she asked, because he didn't trust
easily either. He didn't open up.

Shadows flickered in his eyes.

'I've never given you reason not to trust me.' She echoed
his words.

He shook his head. 'You didn't tell me some very important things before you took what you wanted from me on

that beach. Then you ran,' he said. 'You wouldn't even look back when I called out your name.'

She looked down at the beautiful bed, remembering that fateful afternoon. How overwhelming. How passionate. Maybe in this at least she could be honest.

'You were right,' she whispered quickly. 'I was afraid. Because what we did was...'

'Was what?'

She glanced back up at him. 'Too intense.'

'Was it what we did or what happened after?' he asked. 'You were angry, then I was angry... We won't fight when we're finished today.'

'No?' She half laughed.

'At least I know your name this time. Princess Stella Zambrano De Santis.' His smile was beautiful—that dimpled, genuine, gorgeous smile.

No, there wouldn't be that abrupt end after they'd indulged now. That wouldn't come for months yet. This time there would only be more. Already she was melting.

'Don't be afraid of passion,' he said, reaching for her. 'It is to be enjoyed.'

Passion? Was lust all this was? 'How do people get any work done if they feel like this?'

He laughed and his hands slid to her waist. 'The lucky ones get to indulge in it at their leisure. We're *very* lucky.'

The expression in his eyes stirred that wildness she'd felt on the beach. This was her gorgeous fun-in-the-sun Prince.

'There's nothing to it.' He lifted the veil from her hair and it tumbled in a heap of white on the end of the bed. He looked at her, approval all over him. 'Pretty shoes. Pretty dress.'

So playful. So tempting.

He kissed her, then dropped to his knees, sliding his hands under her skirts.

'What are you doing?'

'What do you think?'

His eyes twinkled as he looked up at her. He knew how instantly this turned her on—seeing him at her feet, so determined to please her. What was there to worry about when he was this generous?

She smiled and closed her eyes, sinking into the sensations he stirred with his intimate caresses. 'I thought we weren't going to rush?' she gasped.

'I can't wait to taste you again. I've been dreaming of it too long.'

He didn't hold back. He pressed hot kisses up her thighs. But he didn't pull back her panties. He teased her through them. She shook all over. Her fingers dug into his shoulders and she gasped, rocking against him.

'Oh, no!' So quick. So intense.

'It's just an orgasm, Stella, get used to it,' he teased. 'You're going to have lots and lots.'

She was going to have one now. His mouth was finally there. Even through the barrier of her cotton briefs she could feel the heat of him, the wicked swirls of his tongue, the maddening rub of his thumb.

'Ohhhhh...' she moaned as it hit. *So good.* She pressed hard on his shoulders to stay upright, but her legs were wobbly.

'And there was me thinking you preferred to stand.' He gripped her hips. 'Always.'

'I can't stand. Don't tease me.'

'But teasing you tastes good.' He kissed her explicitly again.

She wanted this. But it wasn't enough.

As if he'd heard her he rose to his feet and turned her, carefully unfastening the small buttons and then parting her dress. She wore scrupulously plain white cotton panties and a sports bra designed for containment—to minimise bounce, not push for great up-thrust. Nothing decorative. So unsexy.

'I like cotton,' she said stupidly. *Why* hadn't she worn the lacy, frilly things Giulia had silently left on the bed for her?

'I like you.' He tugged her panties down in a couple of swift jerks. 'Bare.'

He undressed her until she wore nothing but the sapphire

he'd chosen for her. He was at her feet, wearing that incredible suit. And he'd stripped her not just of her wedding dress but all her inhibitions.

He kissed every inch of her body. The balmy heat, the breeze wafting through the tunnel, the sound of the sea in her ears was like an erotic dream. But it was Eduardo alone who intoxicated her.

She wanted to see him. She wanted to touch him. Taste. Take. She wanted to feel all of him about her. His strength summoned hers. She instinctively understood that in this they were a match.

'You need to be naked too,' she ordered, feeling her power returning, and the freedom to have him the way she wanted.

He stood and all but ripped off his clothing, until he finally shed the silky black boxers that clung to his muscular thighs, and she openly, avidly gazed at his beautiful body.

'See how you affect me?' he muttered as he climbed onto the thick mattress and pushed her back onto the cool sheets. 'You want to take it, Stella?'

She couldn't wait.

He kissed her again, laughing even as he ravished her with kisses that made her writhe beneath him. His hands traced teasing paths over her bared skin, setting her cells alight, finally finding the secret curves. She arched into his hand.

'Something you want more of?' he teased.

But he gave her only teasing strokes, then finally just the one finger, slipping inside—carefully testing. Too carefully.

She didn't want it as gently as this. She wanted all that raw passion back—like they'd had on the beach. She moved, restless and aching at the slow pace of his fingers.

A smile curved his mouth. 'It doesn't hurt?'

She shook her head, but it was a partial lie. It hurt that he wasn't ferociously claiming her.

'I'm not a virgin any more,' she reminded him.

'I worried later that I'd hurt you,' he said.

'No. It was so good and I felt so wild that I freaked myself out... It wasn't you.'

But it *was* him. He'd been the one to stir up those passions—just as he was stirring them now.

'I like you hot and wet and arching up to me, your body begging for mine,' he muttered, kissing her again. 'But this isn't enough for you, is it?' he asked, his voice roughening.

Could he read her mind? She licked her lips.

'Stella?' He moved his hand, pushing a little deeper, rubbing a little harder.

'No,' she answered, almost angry that he was pushing her to admit it. 'I want more.'

She wanted it as wild and as free as it had been that day on the beach.

'I think you are greedier than you like to admit. Stronger. Ready for rougher. Ready for the rest of me.' He laughed as she moaned. 'And you like it when I talk filth to you.'

She arched as he moved to brace over her, nudging her legs wider and settling between them. Unable to speak. So hot. And, yes, so ready.

'You want me hard?' he asked. 'Fast?' He pressed against her. 'You want me to slam into you, over and over?' He paused, barely inside her, barely giving her enough. But he was so close and she was shaking with need for him.

'Yes,' she begged, curling her fingernails tightly into his hard muscles and trying to pull him deeper. 'Yes. Please. Yes.'

'What else do you want?' he demanded, his breath harsh at her rough caress.

'More.' She didn't want him to stop. Not ever.

'More?' He slid his hand between their bodies, stroking right where she needed it.

'Every. Thing.' She gasped and arched, pulling on his tight muscles. *'More.'* She couldn't get enough. 'You *know.*'

His body tautened and he rolled against her. 'You want everything I have?'

'Yes.' She wanted every part of him.

Every. Single. Part.

'Please,' she begged when he withdrew almost to the tip,

unbearably slowly, while his finger kept up that maddening, delightful stroking. *'Please.'*

'Say my name,' he ordered, rubbing deliciously faster. Then stopping.

She glanced up at him. 'Arrogant. Pirate.' But she would say anything as long as he kept touching her like that. *Do* anything as long as he made her feel this good.

'With you, my pretty captive princess.' His laugh was ragged. 'So determined to fight when really all she wants is for me to—'

And at that moment he did exactly as she wanted—pumping into her, pounding his flesh against hers, every muscle bunching as he moved as hard and as fast as she'd ached for him to do.

She screamed as she rose to meet him, welcoming him, her body slick with sweat and sensuality.

His laugh then was exultant, and triumph glittered from his eyes. But the satisfaction was hers. Her muscles clenched instinctively, trying to lock him in as he thrust over and over, making the friction even more exquisite, sharpening every sense as the crest of the wave crashed over her. Her fingers and toes and everywhere in between flexed and curled as her orgasm hit—such sublime, unbearable pleasure. It was too good to contain. Possibly too fierce to survive. Her scream echoed around the cave.

'Stella!' he shouted as she convulsed in ecstasy, and his own roar of release followed a mere second later. His powerful body shook, his groan stoked her feminine pride and he collapsed into her arms.

This was exactly what she'd wanted.

In the aftermath she lay soft and spread beneath him, unable to move, unable to process anything other than the sheer good feelings reverberating around her body.

As much as her own behaviour had shocked her, she'd thought that day on the beach had been the most intense and exciting moment of her life—something nothing could surpass. She'd been wrong.

'You still with me?' He lifted up onto his elbows and looked down at her.

'That wasn't a rush?' she murmured with a pout. Her inner wanton had truly been woken.

'You were disappointed with that?' His eyes kindled with the challenge.

She didn't answer.

'Voracious woman—you want more already.' He laughed softly as she wriggled under him. 'You think I didn't already know?'

What had she been worried about? That she could have *this*—again and again and again?

He moved slowly, hard again and deep inside her.

Stella moaned. He was right. This could be easy. She could enjoy just this for as long as it lasted.

CHAPTER NINE

IT WAS NO longer blood that ran through Eduardo's veins. It was pure, unadulterated satisfaction. He'd solved this horror situation in the most pleasing way possible. He'd secured the future for several people and he'd just had Stella's physical surrender. Twice.

It wasn't enough already. He wanted her hot and demanding, then panting and pleading, all over again. But he had to take it easy on her, lighten the intensity that she felt—that he felt too. He couldn't launch himself on her again like some insatiable sex-crazed hound.

Food was the perfect displacement activity.

He carefully peeled himself away from her. Sending her a smile, he walked to the silver trolley that had been placed in the corner. It was laden with dishes and drinks—they had enough to keep them comfortable for a few hours yet.

'Are you hungry?' he asked, wincing at his unintended *double entendre*. 'Thirsty?' He poured her a glass of juice.

'Thank you,' she murmured.

He sat on the edge of the bed and watched as she sipped. She looked dazed, slumbrous, her mouth reddened and swollen from his kisses. He could hardly look at her for wanting her. He'd turned into the ever-freaking-ready bunny.

But then he realised that she was sitting too still. And the look on her face...

He cocked his head, studying her. 'What are you thinking?'

The blue in her eyes deepened. So did the colour in her cheeks. Was she feeling the same way he was? Hot? Hungry? Wanting more?

She needed to speak up. He wasn't letting her slide back into silence now.

'You can touch me any time you want—do you under-stand?' He didn't want her to be shy. He wanted her hot, de-manding side unleashed as often as possible. 'Just touch.'

She swallowed. 'Okay.'

'Will you give me the same privilege? Can I touch *you*?'

'Yes.' Her eyes shone brighter. 'Any time you want to. Anywhere.'

He stiffened. Did she know how she pushed his buttons?

'You know I'm likely to take that literally?' he teased, his mind already running away with him. 'Any part of your body. In any place we may be. At any time.'

'I don't just *know* that.' Her small smile had a wicked edge. 'I'm counting on it.'

Her confidence made him hum. And then she suddenly sat up and spread her legs wide...

'Is that an invitation?' he asked huskily.

'It's an order.' Her whisper was sultry.

'That's what you know best, huh? Issuing and obeying or-ders? You really think you can order me around?' He moved up the bed to kneel over her. 'Be warned—I'll do as you say until you scream.'

Making her scream was the most rewarding thing he'd done in ages. So he did it then. Again and then again.

'We can't stay the night down here,' he said with a sorry sigh, stretching out his stiffened muscles several hours later.

'Why not?' she asked drowsily.

'Because the tide will soon be in and our bed might float away.'

Amused, he watched her sit bolt upright and stare at the seawater that was pooling on the farthest side of the bed. Soon enough the tide would wash all the way in.

'Is *that* why we got married when we did?' Something in her eyes softened.

'The time of the ceremony was to match the tide, yes.' It had seemed a good idea last night—a play on her pirate talk. Now he felt a little embarrassed. 'I thought you might like it here.'

'I do.'

She answered so quietly he wasn't quite sure he'd heard her. He combed her hair back from her face with his fingers and looked into her shining eyes. Luminescent. Honest. Giving. That playfulness, that power, was emerging again.

She'd echoed her vows only a few hours ago. At the time he'd been so intent on having her it had been all he could think about. In truth, it was still mostly all he could think about.

I do.

Now those words moved him differently. This woman he barely knew was his *wife*. That wild idea had seemed like the best thing at the time. He'd given in to impulse as always. Duty underlay it, sure, but now an unexpected tension coiled within him.

Wife.

The ramification hit—permanence. Because this couldn't be over in a few days. They'd have to see it through until the birth of the baby and a bit beyond that at least. Pretty much a year, minimum.

Oddly there was no panic—only a hint of regret. For *her*. She had no idea what he'd set her up for.

This island fantasy would end and reality would return. *His* reality. No prince and princess fairy tale, more a 'scary' tale. And he didn't have long to prepare her for what she was going to face.

Stella silently walked barefoot along the beach and then climbed up to the palace. She showered and shrugged on the silk robe left on her bed, then went to find Eduardo.

'Is this your favourite room?' she asked as she explored the trinkets on the shelves in the library.

He nodded. 'I like the view. The books. My chair.'

She chuckled. 'Old man.'

'Let me guess—your favourite room is the gym.' He rolled his eyes.

'Oh, no.' She wrinkled her nose. 'I prefer to be outdoors.'

'So do I—when it's sunny and warm. So sit here.' He gestured to a large seat. 'At least here you can see outside.'

It was a beautiful room. At first glance she'd thought it impersonal and opulent. Now she saw the personal treasures. The old blanket on his favourite chair. It was his nest.

He took the chair beside hers. 'When we get back to San Felipe…' He cleared his throat. 'They're going to ask questions. They're going to ask everything.'

'They?'

'Everyone. So tell me ten things I don't know about you.'

'Seriously?'

'Yes.'

She frowned. 'I thought you knew everything from my personnel file?'

'That's like saying you know everything about me from the gossip magazines.'

Amused appreciation sparkled within her. 'So you're saying we know nothing about each other?'

'What I know about you so far is not something I can share with reporters.' He leaned back, wickedness oozing from his pores. 'We need to fix that. We're under no obligation to answer any media questions, but the public will ask and I refuse to ignore *them*. We need to work on some closed answers.'

'"Closed answers"?' she echoed with a half-laugh. 'You'd be the expert.'

'I mean it, Stella, we need to talk.'

He was suddenly serious. This was the side of Eduardo she knew least.

'What do you want me to do?' she snapped. 'Fill in an online dating questionnaire or something?'

'You've tried online dating?' He raised an eyebrow.

'I was twenty-four and still a virgin. Of *course* I looked into it.'

'I thought you were all about the army?' He cocked his head.

'It was a weak moment.'

'You were lonely?' He sent her an unreadable look. 'Did you go on any dates? It can be risky, meeting an online acquaintance.'

'No riskier than having sex on the beach with a stranger,' she pointed out.

'You knew who I was.' He shrugged.

'But *you* didn't know *me*.'

'I'm working on it,' He grinned shamelessly. 'And now I know you tried online dating.'

'I didn't try it.' She threw up a hand grumpily. 'I thought about it for two minutes. Dismissed it. Because you can't get to know someone just by interviewing them. People give you the answers they think you want to hear.' It was actions that revealed a person. What they did or didn't do.

'But this is all we *can* do in the time we have,' he argued. 'They're going to ask lots of questions.'

'Fine. Then *I'll* ask the questions they're going to ask and you answer them. I'll remember the answers and repeat them as necessary,' she said practically. 'How would we have met?'

'On a beach,' he answered promptly. 'Always the truth, where possible. But it will have to be more than a few months ago. Then we met in private, at the palace. When you were supposedly meeting your father.'

Well, there was a flaw in that story already. 'I didn't come to the palace that often.' About twice since her return to San Felipe.

'That's because Antonio was opposed to us dating. A prince is only supposed to marry a princess, or at least a lady, and you're a soldier—'

'Is he really that uptight?' Stella asked curiously. Or was this as much fiction as the rest of the fairy tale Eduardo was concocting?

He briefly met her eyes, a glint of ironic amusement in his. 'Yes. And you're supposed to be learning about me—not my brother.' His smile tightened and that quirk of softness disappeared into a frown. 'And your father...how will he take it?'

'I don't know,' Stella muttered.

'You're not close?'

'He's a good man.' She avoided answering directly. 'He wants to do what's right. And he's very good at his job.'

Eduardo regarded her for a moment. 'Would you have had him escort you at our wedding?' he asked. 'Will he be hurt by that oversight?'

Oversight? 'You're only wondering about that *now*?' She fiddled with her drink, running a finger around the rim of the glass.

'There are many things of concern right now. Your relationship with your father is only one of them. Should we summon him to my apartment at the San Felipe palace? We can meet him there before seeing Antonio.'

'No.' She didn't want to deal with her father yet, and she certainly didn't want to give *orders* to him. That was his world and no longer hers. If he wanted to know how she was he'd have to step out of service mode.

Neither of those things he ever did.

The truth was she had no real relationship with her father. She'd always disappointed him and he'd dismissed her—in every way possible. There was nothing more she could do.

'Will he back up our story?'

Stella looked up at Eduardo's quiet question, realised he was watching her closely, a frown knitting his eyebrows. She pasted on a cynical smile. 'He would never comment to the media or anyone. He's utterly dutiful.' He'd act the part because he always followed the rules and kept up appearances. 'My father is the perfect emotionless soldier, doing what's best for the greater good.'

He sacrificed the personal in order to serve the Crown Prince. *Every. Time.*

'Is he why you were so determined to succeed in the army?' Eduardo stood up from his chair and paced to the wide windows, looking out at the sunset.

'Of course.' She shrugged and sent her husband a sharp look. 'I've spent my life trying to please him.'

He turned his back to the window and looked down at her. 'Sarcasm doesn't suit you. Anyway, some of what you say is the truth.'

It was. But it wasn't the only truth. 'I loved my job. I wouldn't have stuck at it so long if I hadn't.' She'd loved the freedom and the strength she got from it. She missed it. 'My father was almost fifty when I was born. When my mother died he grieved long and hard, and he was left with a child he had no idea how to raise.' She sighed, suddenly tired. 'He did the best he could.'

He was still her father. She would always defend him. Because even though his distance and disappointment hurt her she still loved him.

'He sent you away?' Eduardo said softly.

Stella frowned. It wasn't that simple. 'He ensured that I had an excellent education and that I came to know my mother's country. That I was well cared for.'

'By boarding school matrons?'

'They understood the needs of a young girl better than he ever could.' She nodded.

'But you came back? To prove yourself in his world?' he persisted.

She paused.

'Because you wanted his approval.' Eduardo stepped towards her and lifted her chin, forcing her to look into his beautiful eyes.

'That's only part of it,' she whispered, hating this analysis. Life was so much more complicated than he made it sound. 'I'm not that pathetic.'

'It's not pathetic. It's normal,' he countered. 'All children crave the love and approval of their parents.'

'Did you?'

'Of course,' he said simply. 'My parents were very proper, and it was all just how it always was…but they were there. They loved us both.'

'And then they died.' She looked at him, guessing that

was a deep-running wound—as it was for her. It was one she could barely think about.

He nodded.

'You're not close to Antonio?'

He paused, and she could almost feel him withdrawing. 'He is very busy. I'm the lucky one. All the weight rests on *his* shoulders.'

'Maybe you're not as carefree as you make yourself out to be.' She studied him. 'You couldn't continue with law…'

He waved his hand dismissively. 'There are limitations on everyone—many others have worse. Some face huge struggles just to get the right to go to school.'

Yes, but that didn't necessarily reduce his personal regret or resentment. 'What else would you have liked to do that you couldn't?' she asked.

There was another hesitation. Then he suddenly straightened, looking her in the eye. 'Your father wouldn't let me serve in the army. Not on active duty.'

That surprised her. 'You wanted to be a soldier?' She knew just how that was—that blanket refusal.

'Trained for two years. Then they said no to anything overseas.'

'They?'

'Your father. My big brother.'

So, no to his first choice of career, limitations in the second. Now he spent his time opening new tourist destinations.

'Are you feeling sorry for me now? The spare heir, living a meaningless, untameable life? *Poor* Prince Eduardo!' He mimicked the headlines that were frequently splashed over glossy magazines.

'Sarcasm doesn't suit *you* either,' she said. 'And there's truth in what you say.'

'So I *am* meaningless and untameable?' He laughed at her expression. 'I'm luckier than so many. And I accept the things I cannot change.'

'Have you ever tried to change them?' she asked. 'Ever

tried to do what everyone says you can't? Thought, *To hell with it... I'll show you*?'

He placed both hands on the arms of her chair and leaned down to gaze into her eyes. A funny smile quirked his lips. 'Perhaps I am not as brave as you.'

'Perhaps you've not found anything you're that passionate about yet.' If he'd really wanted to do it, wouldn't he have fought harder?

'You see?' He released her chair and straightened, reverted back to Prince Charming mode. 'We're getting to know each other already.'

Not enough. She'd always known he felt some constraint in his role—now she wanted to understand more.

'Why did we have Matteo and Giulia as our witnesses?' she asked.

'Because they're the two people I trust most in the world.' He glanced back at her. 'And I don't think the newspapers are going to ask us *that* question.'

'Why not your brother?' She ignored his attempt at deflection. She wanted to know more about their relationship, because while Eduardo had hinted at disharmony he was unquestionably loyal.

For a moment he said nothing. 'Not for this, no.' He turned and shot her a distracting smile, held his hand up as if he were holding a microphone. 'What was it that first drew you to Prince Eduardo?'

Yes, he was very loyal. The fact that he wouldn't discuss Antonio with her drew respect. So she let herself be distracted and smiled back archly. 'You're just fishing for compliments.'

'You're going to be asked that question a lot.'

'No.' She laughed ruefully. 'I'm not. It'll be *you* being asked what you saw in *me*.'

'Your ego is as hungry as mine!' He held his hand out to her and winked. 'Come sit with me and I'll tell you everything.'

But when she stood he stood too, then picked her up and carried her to his bedroom.

* * *

At five the next morning Stella didn't want to drag herself out of bed, but if she didn't she'd lose more than her inhibitions in Eduardo's arms. She'd never felt so wanted, so desired. But aside from sex there was nothing between them. Even the desire couldn't be as strong for him, because if she hadn't got pregnant she'd never have seen him again.

This wasn't real and it wasn't going to last. Just because he was showing her one kind of affection it didn't mean it would become more.

Carefully she slipped out from under his heavy arm and dashed to her bag.

She wasn't afraid of many things—not of travelling to foreign places nor suffering intense physical strain. But what Eduardo made her feel… Sure, it might be easy—but it was still too good. She didn't want to want it too much, because it wasn't lasting.

'What are you doing?' His voice was arctic.

'What does it look like?' She fastened her bra and reached for her trainers.

'You have a problem—you know that?' He groaned and rolled onto his side.

'I like a routine. You'll get used to it.'

She averted her eyes from his tousled gorgeousness. The urge to slide back into bed was almost irresistible. But she *could* resist it—that was the point of this run. To prove to herself that she could control her own desire. She could have him. Or she could choose not to.

To her slight surprise—and disappointment—he didn't try to stop her. Instead he reached for his phone.

She headed for the track.

Yes, soon enough Eduardo would be busy being Prince Eduardo, and when he was sick of the sex she'd have to settle in to her new life as his ex-wife and mother of his child.

She ran the circuit of the small island three times.

He was waiting for her on the step when she returned. He ordered her into the shower. Followed her there. His playfulness made her forget the future and unleashed her own friskiness again. She leaned into his touch.

She'd proved herself, right? She could turn her back and take time out from him whenever she wanted. She could say no to him.

She just didn't want to right now.

CHAPTER TEN

EDUARDO WALKED TOWARDS where Stella was reading on the sofa in the library. The level of scrutiny she would soon face would be unprecedented. He wished he could keep her here, but already there had been calls and questions from San Felipe palace officials. Eduardo couldn't hold them off much longer.

He'd thought she would open up more, but it turned out that his wife was reticent as he. She talked about books, movies, food and places she'd travelled to; she had wild, gorgeous sex with him, but she offered little detail on anything too personal.

And now he didn't just *need* to know more—he wanted to.

'What do you do for fun?' He wrapped his arm around her ankles and lifted her legs so he could steal in beside her on the sofa. 'Or what *did* you do before I introduced you to the delights of rampant lust?'

'Very funny.'

'Well? What?' Chuckling, he massaged her sleek calves. 'What did you do when you were on leave? Don't tell me you just went for runs all the time?'

Beneath his hands her muscles stiffened. 'I *like* running.'

Clearly. She'd left him in bed at some awful hour this morning and gone for her laps around the island. Her discipline and determination irritated him. And turned him on.

'What else do you like?'

'Working. I like my job.'

'Okay, let's do this another way.' He stopped touching her—it was the only way he could keep thinking. 'What if for the next twenty-four hours we could go anywhere and do anything? Tell me—where do we go and what do we do?'

She just looked at him.

'Broadway, New York…?' he suggested with a waggle of his eyebrows. 'A shopping spree in Paris and all the rides at Disneyland…? Give me a destination and I can make it happen.'

'You're talking hypothetically?'

'No. If you want to go to LA we can go to LA. The jet is on standby.'

Her eyebrows arched. 'Just like that?'

'Yes.' He shrugged, a little embarrassed by her amazement. 'So, what do you want to do?'

She glanced out of the window and down the length of the small coast. 'I like the privacy *here*.'

He was pleased that she loved the island. 'So do I.' He studied her, wishing like hell that he could see into her mind. 'How about we do something *I* think is fun?'

She turned back and sent him an arch, ultra-sarcastic look. 'Haven't we been doing that day and night?'

Yes, and it still wasn't enough. But the public's appetite for information on her was going to be voracious. He had to prepare them both.

'You think that's the only kind of fun I know how to have?'

Her chin lifted at the challenge in his voice and her eyes gleamed. 'Okay, then—show me Prince Eduardo–style fun.'

'As my Princess wishes…' He inclined his head, mocking her formal address.

'I'm not a princess,' she muttered.

'To me you are.' He leaned forward and kissed her, delighting in the shiver that shook her.

'You're a silver-tongued pirate,' she breathed, but she kissed him back.

He broke away before his plans went awry. 'There was me, thinking you *liked* what I do with my tongue.'

'Still so arrogant.' Her eyes gleamed like stunning, sleepy sapphires.

'And you like it.' But he wasn't letting her derail him with her wiles. Not this time.

Half an hour later he led her down a small boat ramp and handed her a life jacket from the pile of gear his aides had left for them.

Stella had already spotted the yacht.

'What kind of boat is *that*?' She looked at the small, sleek beauty, roped to the moorings.

'She's a Tempest. She's vintage. Even starred in a few regattas a while back. Her name is *Miranda*.' He laughed at his own silly pride.

'Of course it is.' Stella leaned out and peered onto the deck. 'But we're not going to get shipwrecked, right?'

'Not unless you steer us onto the rocks.' He fastened his jacket, amused that she'd got the Shakespeare reference.

'You usually sail it alone?'

'Yes, but it's a two-crew vessel. You up for it?' He didn't know why he'd bothered asking—she'd already stepped on board. 'You've sailed before?'

She shook her head. 'Kayaked, rowed, but never sailed.'

'Then let's do it.'

She was a natural athlete and a quick learner, and it wasn't long before she was anticipating his instructions and they were working as a team. Her physicality matched his, and he pushed her more than he'd planned to. The yacht skimmed over the water. Time flew, as it always did for him when he was sailing.

'You love it, don't you?' She turned to look at him, breaking the silence.

'Yes.' He couldn't tear his gaze from her. She was radiant. Soft when it counted, strong when she needed to be. And *so* into it.

'I feel like this when I'm running.' She glanced up at the sails.

'Like what?'

'Free. Powerful.'

And she didn't feel like that the rest of the time? She should. She was amazingly powerful.

'And at the mercy of the elements,' she added with a laugh as a spray of water got her.

'You've not had enough?' he asked. 'Not feeling seasick at all?'

'No,' she answered swiftly.

'And no morning sickness?'

'No.' Something flashed on her face as she shut down the pregnancy talk.

'You must do *something* other than running for fun?' he asked, trying to remain relaxed. But her self-containment was irritating the hell out of him.

'I do lots,' she said. 'Anything outdoors—walking, cycling—'

'Sex on the beach...' he interpolated.

'That too, yes.' She owned it with a glint in her eye.

'So why me? Why not some guy in your battalion?' His body thrummed. 'Why did you wait so long and then say yes so quickly?'

'This was your ploy? To take me miles out into the ocean and launch twenty questions at me?'

He let silence do its thing.

She gripped a rope more tightly. 'Why should I tell you all my secrets when you won't tell me yours?'

Did she think this was some game of chicken? Couldn't she understand he was trying to *help* her?

'What do you want to know?' he demanded. 'Ask me anything.'

'What is it that you don't want to tell me?'

She didn't shout. She just asked softly—all wide eyes and petite strength. And she got to him in a way no one else ever had.

'You really know how to torture a man.'

And she really knew how to challenge him.

She frowned. 'Tell me the worst thing you've ever done, aside from getting me pregnant.'

'That's not the worst thing I've ever done,' he snapped. 'We're growing a baby. That's amazing.'

Her cheeks lost colour. 'Well, what can you tell me that would make me like you less?'

'So you *like* me?'

'That would make me *want* you less.'

At that admission something broke within him. He wanted to know her thoughts. Because what she thought suddenly mattered.

'I let my brother down,' he said bluntly. 'Many times. Too impulsive…too unreliable. Too hot-headed—'

'You're not that bad,' she interrupted. 'You're just under greater scrutiny than most. Everyone screws up.'

'Not the way I have.' Soft words tumbled from him. The culmination of hurt and guilt and desperation to stop his mistakes spiralling into a mess meant he couldn't hold back. 'I was studying in England when our parents were killed.'

Her eyes widened, but she didn't say anything at his change in tone.

Eduardo couldn't look at her any more, so he looked across the blinding blue water instead.

'Antonio needed to concentrate on his coronation. I wanted to return home to help, but he refused. He said it would be better for me to stay studying abroad while he handled it. He didn't want to have to worry about me.'

He glanced at her when she made a small sound and shook his head at the pity he read in her eyes.

'Matteo was with me. I wasn't alone. Not the way Antonio was. His girlfriend, Alessia, was already studying at Cambridge when I got there. They'd been secretly engaged since school. He wouldn't let her come home either. He delayed announcing their engagement. He didn't think it right to celebrate so soon after our parents' death.'

'I know about Alessia,' Stella said softly.

Everyone knew about Alessia now. And that was Eduardo's fault.

'What is it that you know,' he asked bitterly. 'That she got sick? That Antonio buried his heart with her when she died?' The old guilt and helplessness surged inside him. 'Do you know *why* you know all that?'

Stella waited silently. And, stupidly, that made him madder.

'Alessia hadn't told Antonio how bad it was because she didn't want to bother him at such a difficult time. She swore me to secrecy and I promised her I wouldn't tell him.'

'You cared about her?'

'She was the big sister I'd never had.' He nodded. 'The one person who made Antonio smile. He was always serious, always burdened, but she brought him joy. And he pushed her away. I was so angry with him.'

He hadn't been able to understand why Antonio had kept her at a distance, and he'd been angry when his brother had pushed him away too. Because he'd been too young, too impulsive, not really necessary—which was pretty much the sum total of his life. 'Special' but not needed.

'I didn't tell him and I should have. I should have made him come and see her.'

Stella frowned. 'What happened?'

He regretted this already. But he saw the look in Stella's eyes and the words fell from him anyway. 'I was dating a girl from my law class. She saw me with Alessia and was jealous. I told her the truth—that Alessia was Antonio's fiancée and that she was sick, and that was why I was visiting her. But I hadn't realised just how sick Alessia was. And then Antonio learned that his fiancée was dying through the media.'

'Because your girlfriend sold the story?'

The look of outrage and disgust on her face made him smile bitterly. 'Alessia refused to see him, but he got in to see her anyway. She refused to marry him. She couldn't give him heirs. She was too ill. He said he didn't want children—he wanted her for as long as they had left. But she still refused. She sent him back to San Felipe and in the end he had to go. He had to rule. She died a few weeks later.'

He reached past Stella to steer the yacht back on course. 'He won't marry now, won't have children. He promised that to Alessia and he's determined to keep it true. That is his decision. Duty above all else.' He glanced up at the flapping sail and pulled on a rope. 'He could have had a chance with her…even just more *time*. But I let him down by not telling him. And then by talking to someone I thought I could trust.'

'It wasn't your fault,' she said. 'You should have been able to trust her. Antonio must have understood that.'

'Antonio was lost in his own grief and I just made things worse for myself. That was my "playboy prince" period.' He grimaced. He'd given in to a downward spiral of meaningless sex and parties. His university daze.

'What made you stop?'

'It wasn't fun any more.'

He'd got bored, unhappy, *lonely*. He'd come home and apologised to an unmoved Antonio and he had been trying to redeem himself ever since. But he was still bound by the limitations his meaningless title imposed.

He sighed. 'Shall we see how fast we can make her go?'

'Yes.'

Eduardo loved fast. So did Stella.

Those headlines she'd read—*Search for San Felipe's brides—who will heal Antonio? Who will tame Eduardo?* She'd thought it was all glossy marketing speak to help sell the romance of the islands to tourists, but it was based in truth. Eduardo was everything she'd imagined—full of vitality and energy and passion. But he was also full of anger and hurt, and she'd never expected to ache because of that.

Her leg pressed close to Eduardo's as they sat side by side on the very edge of the vintage yacht, half hanging over the water as they raced as fast as they could.

'I'd missed out on a promotion,' she confessed. 'That day I met you on the beach.'

He looked at her.

'I was so angry and so alone and I…' She drew in a deep breath. 'You didn't know me. I wasn't the usual challenge to you—the tough one all the guys placed bets on. I wasn't the

General's forbidden daughter. I wasn't *any*one. I was just a girl and you were—' She broke off.

'The pirate Prince?'

'You were fun and a…a rogue. And—'

'You thought you knew me?' He shook his head. 'There's more to me than that. Just as there is more to you than being the General's daughter.'

'Yes,' she muttered—she was learning that about him. 'But back then I just wanted a moment for *me*.'

'Only now you're paying quite the price?'

She didn't like the sombre expression that had entered his eyes. 'A boatload of trouble, you think?' she teased, pleased when she saw his amusement sparkle back. 'Are we going to land on that island?'

She sat up and put out her hand to shade her eyes, realising they were getting closer and closer to a land mass.

She rested for the next twenty minutes as Eduardo sailed the small yacht right up to an ancient wooden jetty and leapt to secure it.

He grinned at her and held out his hand to help her up. 'Come on.'

'Where are we?' She stretched and started walking.

'A tiny town on the coast of Sardinia.'

Stella gaped. 'We sailed *that* far?'

'We've been going for hours.' He pulled a phone from his pocket and, yanking it out of the dry bag he'd stored it in, walked along the dock with her.

'No wonder I'm starving.' She jogged ahead, on the look-out for the nearest eatery in this very small town.

'Stella—'

'Come on—I'm famished!' she called as he lagged behind her.

She spotted a small, grimy-looking café. The 'Closed' sign was up, but she went inside the open doorway anyway, hoping to convince the proprietor to make them a small snack.

'I'm sorry,' she said rapidly in Italian to the worn-looking woman behind the counter. 'Would you mind—?' She broke off as sheer amazement and then blushing wonder washed over the woman's face.

As the woman dropped into a deep curtsy Stella turned to look at Eduardo, walking up behind her. Before her eyes he was transformed from her windswept, sexy companion to 'the Prince'—the suave, charming man on all those magazine covers. But his smile, while still gorgeous, was slightly set, and that tiny dimple had disappeared. Small changes she wouldn't have noticed before.

And now she read the brief apology in his eyes.

But *she* felt sorry—because she'd broken their brief private peace. *Everyone* knew who he was. Everyone *changed* in his presence. He was 'different'.

As the General's daughter, in the army she'd been 'different' too. Their birth circumstances stood them apart from others, and they each had to play a part.

But hers had been nothing on his. Now she started to understand the strain and isolation he felt when appearing in public. From this one woman's overwhelmed reaction she saw what it must be like for him, walking into those galleries or gardens or concert halls filled with people craning their necks to have a look at him?

And he did it alone. His brother was too busy and aloof, doing 'important' Crown Princely things.

But now—at least for a little while—Eduardo had her at his side. Suddenly she didn't want to let him down. She wanted to play her new part as well as she could. Except her clothes were wet, and no doubt her hair was wild.

She should have thought before sprinting into the small town and flinging herself into the first café she'd found. But it was too late. The woman promised absolute discretion and bustled away to fix them some food.

'I should have realised you would be hungry.' Eduardo fetched a chair for Stella and waited until she was seated. 'I'm sorry.'

'We lost track of time, sailing.' She smiled. 'It was fun.'

That beautiful, intimate smile flashed on his face, but it

disappeared almost instantly when he caught sight of something over her shoulder.

Stella turned.

It was a young child, peeking from behind the café counter. Stella turned back to see Eduardo waving the girl over with a conspiratorial wink. Two minutes later he was laughing at the manageress when she brought their dishes over and came to apologise.

'It's okay,' Eduardo assured them. 'We would love to talk with you.'

'You're Prince Eduardo from San Felipe,' the girl said.

'Yes.'

'Who's she?' With the unashamed curiosity of the young, the girl stared at Stella.

'She's my princess,' Eduardo answered.

The little girl's eyes widened. 'Did you *make* her a princess?'

'Yes.'

'Can you make *me* a princess?'

Eduardo laughed lightly. 'I'm sorry, sweetheart, I had only one crown to give and I gave it to her.'

Like a heat-seeking missile the older woman's gaze locked on Stella's hand. Her jaw dropped as she clocked the heavy sapphire and the gold band. Stella turned to Eduardo, but he was too busy talking to the small girl to notice. Yeah... he didn't just win the hearts of every *woman* who laid eyes on him, but every person who spent more than two seconds with him.

'You've made their day,' Stella said softly when the woman returned to the kitchen with the giggling little girl running ahead.

'It's not me,' Eduardo answered drily. 'It's the title. It's my job.'

She lifted her fork and pointed it at him. 'Your brother is a prince too, and he doesn't get that reaction from people. It's *you*. Not your title.'

He sipped some water.

'You don't believe me?' She jabbed her fork harder in the air. 'You have such power. You can bring people to everyone's attention.'

'Are *you* prepared for everyone's attention?' he asked in a low voice.

'Sure. Bring it on. I'm not afraid of a challenge.' She eyeballed him, hot tension swirling between them again.

'No. Not of *issuing* them.'

They ate quietly, hungrily. It was simple, but delicious.

'Come on. Let's use some of my supposed power, shall we?' Eduardo said once Stella had lowered her fork, utterly replete. 'I think they're on to us anyway.'

'You think...?' Stella sighed.

He stood and talked quietly to the woman. The woman's face lit up like fireworks and she scurried to the kitchen. Seconds later she returned, phone in hand.

Startled, Stella looked at Eduardo. He simply smiled his best 'Prince Eduardo' smile.

'Are you sure?' Stella whispered out of the side of her mouth as they posed for a photo.

Eduardo merely put his arm around her waist and drew her closer. 'Smile, my Princess. This is the first of many.'

'But she'll probably put it on social media in seconds.'

'She'll have snapped some pictures in secret anyway— it's better to give her permission to make the most of it. And it won't be social media. I'm sure she's savvy enough to sell them.'

Stella turned to look up into his eyes and saw the hint of bitterness. He expected not to trust the woman. Expected that his private moments would be sold even when someone had promised him they wouldn't. Just as his ex-girlfriend had sold his secret about Alessia.

He didn't trust anyone. Yet he'd told her about Alessia and his own involvement. Did that mean he trusted *her*?

For a half-second she hoped so. But then she remembered that he'd been savvy enough to ensure she'd signed a contract—binding her to silence. Now she understood why he'd felt the need to.

'It will become the most popular restaurant on the island,' Stella said as they left the woman and the girl waving from the café.

'For a while.' He nodded.

For a long time, she'd bet.

Eduardo looked at his watch, his eyes narrowing. 'Come on, we need to get going.' He turned away from the marina and started walking quickly.

'We're not going back in *Miranda*?'

'It would take too long and we'd get lost at sea.' He took her hand. 'I phoned for the plane. It's here now, and a car is on its way to take us to the airfield. We'll meet it along this road in a minute or so.'

He'd *what*?

'Plane? Where are we flying to?' Stella hurried to keep pace.

'San Felipe,' he answered briefly. 'It's only a short flight—we'll use the baby jet.'

A laugh bubbled from her. 'That's what you call it?'

'It's not as big as Antonio's.' He sent her a look as a sleek car pulled in alongside them.

'Never mind.' She patted his shoulder soothingly before she climbed into the back seat. 'You don't have to prove yourself to *me*.'

'I know,' he muttered with a wicked smile, his tone mimicking her earlier whisper. 'Because I've already captured your heart.'

He thought it was a joke, but his words held too much truth for her comfort.

Ten minutes later they walked across an airstrip to board the waiting plane. Eduardo might consider it a 'baby', but it was the biggest private jet she'd ever been in. All luxurious fittings and gleaming paintwork. But as the powerful engines were fired up she couldn't relax and enjoy it. She'd thought she'd have more time to prepare before facing mainland San

Felipe. She'd thought she have another night alone with him on their secret island.

'Under no circumstances are we to be disturbed.'

She sank into one of the plush chairs as Eduardo instructed his staff.

'Of course, Your Highness.' The man disappeared through the door that Stella guessed led to the cockpit.

She belted up for take-off as Eduardo took the seat opposite hers. She refused to meet his eyes but knew he was watching her relentlessly. She knew what he wanted. Mile High Club, here she came. She'd be willing if she wasn't so worried about what was going to happen when they landed back on solid ground.

'Do you play cards?' He sprawled back in the seat opposite her as the plane levelled out. 'Doesn't every soldier carry a deck?'

'Not all. *I* do. But I prefer Patience to poker. I'm guessing you're a poker player?'

'And *I'm* guessing you prefer a challenge of skill and strategy over chance and fate?'

'You're a quick learner too,' she acknowledged.

'Observant.'

He wasn't just a pretty prince…

'What about a board game instead?' He stood and opened one of the storage compartments.

'You have *board games* on the plane?' Somewhat bemused, she watched him pick out the third box from a stack. 'It's not all lap-dancing flight attendants and whisky?'

'Maybe later—if you're lucky,' he drawled.

'You'd give me a lap dance?' She gazed up at him, for a moment indulging in a vision of him slowly stripping his formal uniform from his body.

He turned and his eyes locked on hers—clashed in a slam of suggestion and want. He actually flushed. Heat burst within her. The plane was suddenly very, very *hot*. His eyebrows were raised and she looked away, burning up.

He unfolded the playing board on the table between their

chairs. He handed her a pile of plastic pieces and sat back down in his seat. 'See if you can defeat my army and we'll negotiate.'

Swallowing, she put one of the plastic toys upright on the board with a click, pushing away the unruly X-rated images in her head. 'Soldiers, huh?'

'It's the closest I'm allowed to get to any battlefront,' he muttered, faux mournfully.

'You know you can play with this soldier any time?' she murmured, still enjoying the way she'd made the colour in his cheeks deepen with her lap-dance request.

'I intend to—once I've conquered her every last defence.' The truly relaxed, flirtatious Eduardo had returned. 'I'm thinking lap-dancing and whisky...'

But they played the board game for the duration of the flight. It didn't take long for him to run through the rules and for her to grasp the idea. He was a good tactician, but so was she. Both advanced quickly to secure large tracts of the board. Both claimed territory the other had held. Both took prisoners. Both held the board steady on the table through the descent. And once the plane had landed and slowed to a stop Eduardo met her gaze with a belligerent edge to his jaw.

'I'm not leaving until you have capitulated control of the south-west quarter,' he said.

'Well, I'm not leaving until I have your ultimate surrender,' she answered smugly.

'You do not do things by halves, do you?' He shook the dice furiously. 'And you never give in.'

'As if you do!'

Their eyes met again, the frisson of tension building. She liked it that he was as determined, as competitive, as dominant as she. She liked so damn much about him. And the more she got to know him, the more she liked. Which made her even more determined to beat him—to have something over him, just the once.

She had no idea how much time passed before his phone buzzed. He ignored it the first time. And the second. It wasn't until the seventh consecutive buzz of the device that he finally reacted.

With an irritated sigh he read the messages and then looked up, his expression grim. 'We have to go to the palace—now.'

He sent a quick text reply and less than a minute later the aircraft door was opened.

The back of her neck prickled as she saw the uniformed attendants. 'How long have we been sitting here?'

'Too long,' he admitted wryly.

She stood and realised he was right. 'I'm stiff.' She considered herself to be fitter than most, but the sailing had used muscles she didn't know existed.

'If you're lucky—' Eduardo paused at the top of the stairs and turned back to send her a heated look '—I'll give you a massage when we get home.'

'Don't forget the lap dance.'

She stepped out after him. He took her hand and walked her into the terminal. More uniformed staff whisked them along a private corridor and out to a waiting limousine before she could believe it. Her smile faded when she saw Matteo sitting in the car waiting for them, an iPad in his hand.

'Problem?' Eduardo asked as he opted to sit beside his lawyer.

'I'm sorry, Eduardo.' Matteo glanced back at the screen. 'I tried, but there was no way to hold back the flood.'

Stella's blood iced.

CHAPTER ELEVEN

STELLA SAID NOTHING Eduardo grabbed the iPad and stared at the screen. He swiped it a few times, scrolling down. Then he looked at her. Without saying anything he tilted the tablet so she could see what he'd been reading.

Eduardo's Secret Soldier Bride!

The headline was emblazoned across the top and there was a picture beneath... Shock rolled through Stella.

'How did they get that photo?' All the amusement of the past few hours disappeared. 'Someone leaked it?'

Eduardo was like granite. Expressionless. Unmoved.

'Not Giulia?'

'No.' Eduardo shook his head. 'She has been in service with my family for decades.'

'All her life?'

'All mine,' he replied shortly. 'She was my nanny.'

'Really?' She was momentarily diverted, touched that he'd wanted his old carer present at his marriage. And now she understood why Giulia had worked so quietly and endlessly to help her get ready. The woman had a soft spot for the spoilt second son. 'Then who?'

He frowned and turned away. 'I will find out. But it does not matter—it was going to become public anyway.'

Stella looked at the photograph, scarcely recognising herself. She was standing just outside the chapel, at the moment when Giulia had gone to check all was ready. They must have Photoshopped it because she looked soft and pretty, and so happy, holding that bouquet of roses up with a small smile curving her lips.

She scrolled down and read the text. Her name. Her history. Her entire service record, there for everyone to read. Horrified, she scanned the words.

'How did they find all this out?' she asked. 'How did this happen?' She squinted at the screen. 'Do they know about—?'

'It is not mentioned.' Eduardo guessed her concern and answered, flicking a glance at Matteo, who was busy scrolling through another iPad. 'I've checked the other papers—they've picked up on the story but there is nothing.'

It was all suddenly very real. And yet it wasn't real.

'It says we've been in love for ages.' She could hardly speak for the shock. 'That we fell in love in the palace. That you met me there because of my father...' The Prince and the General's daughter. Star-crossed lovers whose relationship was forbidden by the Crown Prince...

'You might want to hit Refresh,' Matteo said apologetically.

Stella stared as new pictures were loaded onto the screen. There were the ones from the café. And then pictures of them walking across the tarmac from the 'baby jet'. Pictures taken only five minutes ago. They looked dishevelled, in their water-stained shorts and tee shirts, her hair in a loose, wild ponytail.

The headline made a meal of them having spent an *hour* on the tarmac before disembarking. They'd speculated that it had been so that the new Princess could make herself pretty before being snapped by the paparazzi... But then she and Eduardo had stepped out and she'd looked like *that*. Apparently it was 'obvious' that they'd spent the time engaged in 'other pursuits'. But she knew the flush she'd worn wasn't from orgasmic pleasure but board-game victory.

Before her eyes crude joke after crude joke filled the 'comments' section.

'I must see Antonio,' Eduardo said grimly. 'Release the wedding pictures,' he said to Matteo. 'They will counteract these.'

'Wedding pictures?' Stella asked faintly.

'Matteo took some inside the chapel,' he answered distractedly, scrolling through the images again.

He had? She'd not been aware of anything but Eduardo in that moment.

And now Eduardo was busily tapping out emails. Wham-bam—back to business. She had to remember that this marriage was little more than another of his business deals. They'd signed the paperwork and everything.

This was not a fairy tale. This was not for ever. Their fantasy escape was over.

CHAPTER TWELVE

STELLA STRODE QUICKLY, trying to match Eduardo's pace through the vast gilded corridors to his private rooms. Even though she'd spent chunks of her childhood in the immense palace, she now found it forbidding, and she'd certainly never been into the Princes' wing before. Now she'd learnt that Antonio had one floor, Eduardo another, and there were formal reception rooms on the floor between the two, where they'd meet.

'There's a gym, but I will have a treadmill brought up to our rooms so you can have greater privacy,' said Eduardo as he opened a door, waving away the servants who'd materialised.

'I prefer to run outside.'

'You can't here,' Eduardo said flatly, closing the door behind them but not stepping further into the room. 'It isn't safe, and I don't want the paparazzi getting pictures of you pounding the pavement.'

'That isn't what princesses *do*?' she asked wryly. 'It seems I have a lot to learn.'

'You'll do fine.' He met her sharp look. 'I already know you're a fast learner.'

The atmosphere smouldered between them but the constraints niggled at her. 'You'd better tell me what else I can and cannot do.'

'Just continue to be your discreet, dutiful self and you'll be fine.'

She scowled, but Eduardo had already turned away.

'I must see him,' Eduardo said distractedly. 'Shower and change. I'll come for you in half an hour.'

Stella walked through his expansive apartment. It was beautifully decorated but impersonal—there was none of the 'stuff' that had littered the shelves of the library on Secreto Real.

In the sumptuous bedroom there was an adjoining dressing room. Her clothes, cleaned and pressed, hung on the rack. There were other clothes too—the outrageously expensive ones, purchased especially by a servant, that she'd never worn. The ones that would make her *look the part*. She turned her back on them. She wasn't going to pretend to be anything other than herself when she dealt with the Crown Prince.

It wasn't Eduardo who fetched her forty-five minutes later, but one of the liveried staff.

The second she walked in she knew things weren't going well. The brothers stood on opposite sides of the room. Eduardo had that fiery, ruthless look he'd had the day he'd announced they were marrying. Antonio had no expression at all. They shared much—the same colouring, similar stature—but where Eduardo's eyes were hot, Antonio's were ice.

'You are Carlos's daughter?' Antonio addressed her.

'Yes.'

He didn't look at her—he looked *through* her. It was like being dunked in an Antarctic dive-hole.

'May I offer my congratulations?'

Stella couldn't tell if he was being sarcastic or not. He was expressionless. Bloodless. So unlike his brother.

'All of Europe will wish to do the same,' Antonio added. 'So the ball scheduled for Saturday shall become a marriage celebration—'

'Antonio, no.' Eduardo interrupted him, moving to stand beside Stella. 'You're not still planning—?'

'It has been planned for months, as you well know,' Antonio said brusquely. 'Guests have been arriving all week while you've been "ill".'

'But she's not ready—'

'I am cast as the evil older brother in this scenario you have created.' Antonio turned his icicle eyes onto his brother. 'I will not remain so.'

Eduardo glared back. 'Antonio—'

'The ball has been planned for months—or do you expect us *all* to act rashly and ruin the happiness and expectations of others? You have deprived the nation of a royal wedding. This celebration is the least you can give the people,' Antonio went on, his cold fury now evident. 'She has less than forty-eight hours to get "ready".' Antonio sent her another dismissive glance. 'But the sapphire, a dress and a smile are all that will be necessary.'

Didn't he like her jeans? What a cold, patronising jerk to relegate her to 'decorative only' status.

'I think you'll find Stella has more to offer than that,' Eduardo answered, before she had a chance to breathe.

Antonio's eyebrows lifted almost imperceptibly, giving him a supercilious look. 'You should have come to me first.'

'Even you have to agree this solves several problems. Leave it, Antonio, it is done,' Eduardo answered. 'I promise we'll parade beautifully and dutifully at the ball. We won't let you down.'

It was obvious Antonio thought they already had.

'You will attend the pre-ball functions tonight and tomorrow as well,' Antonio ordered. 'But to maintain the "mystery" and heighten anticipation, the ball will be Stella's first formal public appearance.'

Stella's pulse tripped as Antonio issued his wintry instructions. She recognised that look in his eyes. It was the same one she saw in her father's. She was a *disappointment*. He didn't want Eduardo to have married her. Yet again she was not 'right'. Not for her job. Not for this relationship.

Was Antonio's disapproval because she wasn't nobility? Her father was the first General who had earned his position through *work*—not via his birth, name and lineage. Did that make her unworthy of the wretched sapphire Eduardo had hung around her neck?

Or was it just *her*?

Eduardo's hand was firm on her back, guiding her out of the room. She didn't bother saying goodbye to the Crown

Prince, as protocol and common politeness dictated. She was too hurt.

'Please excuse my brother,' Eduardo said briefly, but he didn't offer any explanation for Antonio's frostiness. 'I'm sorry, I need to leave you alone again for a while. Ask Giulia if you need anything.'

'Of course.'

It wasn't 'a while' that he was gone. It was hours. She dined alone in his apartment, waited up, but in the end sleep overcame her before he returned.

'Stella…' He woke her in the morning with a whisper and a kiss.

She opened her eyes and found herself wrapped in his arms.

'I'd better get on that treadmill,' she groaned.

'You'd better get on me first.'

His gaze drilled into her. His body invaded. Devastated. It was so good. It so wasn't enough. So much for easy.

As soon as she'd recovered some energy she left him in the bed and went to maintain her routine. She would resist when she wanted to.

She was twenty minutes into her time on the treadmill when he placed an iPad on the stand in front of her.

'My assistant has prepared a dossier on many of tomorrow night's guests. Photos, names, positions.'

'That's useful,' she puffed as she jogged and swiped the screen. 'Thank you.'

'I have other duties I must fulfil,' he said, a hint of apology in his eyes. 'I'll be back later tonight.'

Already she understood that he meant very, *very* late.

Was this to be her future? To be left locked in the palace with nothing to do but pretty herself for a ball and grow a baby, and at night be a sexual plaything for her insatiable husband? Sure, she was every bit as insatiable as he, but this wasn't the life she wanted. She wanted her *control* back.

So she'd control *this*. She knew how to fight. She just needed different armour from her usual. Antonio had been right—in part. At the very least she needed 'the sapphire, a dress and a smile' and the ability to remember a couple dozen names and faces.

Because she wasn't going to fail.

As she ran on the treadmill she memorised the names and faces. Then she called Giulia and requested a beautician and a hairdresser to be summoned for later in the day. She'd damn well become the Princess San Felipe had wanted for so long.

'Can you get Dr Russo to come and see me at his convenience as well?' she asked Giulia, trying to sound as relaxed as she had when she'd asked for the beautician.

'Of course.'

The doctor arrived within twenty minutes. Because of that swift timing, Stella was certain Giulia knew about her condition.

'Is everything all right, Your Highness?' Dr Russo bowed as he entered the private sitting room.

'Please call me Stella.' She gestured towards the chairs. 'I'm sorry to trouble you, I just wanted to talk to you about my pregnancy.'

'No trouble.' He sat down. 'What did you want to discuss?'

She curled her hands into small fists, hiding the dampness of her palms, and smiled. 'It sounds stupid, but where are my symptoms? I haven't had any morning sickness, I haven't been particularly tired, I've got no cravings... It's like it's not real.'

What if it wasn't growing properly? Shouldn't she hate the smell of coffee or something?

To her relief, the doctor didn't laugh.

'Perhaps you're one of the lucky few,' he suggested calmly.

'Or perhaps there's something wrong.'

He regarded her steadily. 'Why would there be anything wrong?'

She hesitated. Her throat tightened. But this was the one person she *had* to speak to. 'My mother died a few hours after giving birth to me.'

His eyes widened and the professional smile faded.

'I didn't mention it on the island because I didn't want to panic anyone,' she added quickly.

'Do you know any details?' he asked carefully.

'I think she had some kind of haemorrhage. My father doesn't speak of it.' He never spoke of her mother. He never spoke to Stella about anything personal or important. 'I don't know much else.'

Dr Russo remained calm. 'You were born in San Felipe?'

'The main hospital—yes.'

'Then, with your permission, I'll check the records there. And we will get a scan arranged for you as soon as possible.'

'Please... After the ball.' She needed to know. To understand and prepare.

'Of course.' Dr Russo suddenly lifted his case onto the table. 'I brought a Doppler with me today. It's a small device we can use to listen to your baby's heartbeat. You're far enough along in your pregnancy for us to be able to do that. Would you like to hear your baby?'

For a second Stella's own heart stopped, then started pounding. 'Okay.'

Fleetingly she wished Eduardo was there, but he was busy. And she didn't want to tell him about her mother. Or her fears.

She lay on the sofa, her shirt lifted. The doctor switched the small machine on and held the wand to her stomach.

'It sounds like hoofbeats,' she said, her eyes filling.

'It sounds strong.' Dr Russo looked pleased. 'And *you* are very strong. I will research, but what caused your mother's haemorrhage probably isn't going to be hereditary. You will be in the hospital here, with the world's best specialists. The most important thing is for you to relax and enjoy your pregnancy and this special time with all the celebrations.'

Enjoy it? She was too scared.

'Have you talked to Eduardo about your concerns?' he asked quietly.

'Of course,' Stella lied.

'Good.' The doctor nodded. 'Be assured, your baby is well. I'll follow up soon. You will have the best care, Your Highness.'

'I know.' But her mother had been in the same hospital. She'd had the best care too. And she hadn't made it.

After the doctor had left she sat down to look over the dossier about the guests once more. But in her mind those heartbeats echoed. The baby was *real*. And it was doing okay. But what would happen when the rest of the world found out?

Pretty pictures from the wedding wouldn't be enough to stop people talking—they'd say it was a shotgun wedding. They'd say she'd trapped him into it. They'd say so much more, so much worse.

No matter what she did, it wasn't going to be good enough. It never was.

Eduardo hated that Stella left their bed so early every morning. He tried to tease her into staying, but while she'd happily have sex with him again, she still left the bed immediately after.

He showered and quickly dressed. He had to attend the opening of a new football academy this morning. before another appearance in the afternoon. And then there was the ball tonight. Right back to the usual busy schedule.

She was at the treadmill already, glaring at the screen, watching her pace and distance as if she were wishing they were real miles taking her far from here. The iPad was in position too, and she swiped the screen with fierce movements.

'What are you so angry about?' he asked, reaching out to flick the 'stop' switch on the treadmill.

'Nothing.' She didn't look at him.

'I once asked you not to lie to me,' he said softly. He wanted to know what was eating her up—he wanted her to turn and talk to him.

She put her hands on the rails and sighed. 'They'll stare. They'll stare and they'll judge. I have to prove myself.' She lifted her head and he saw anguish and anger in her eyes. 'And I *never* do. It's *never* enough.'

A rush of protectiveness erupted within him. But he put his hands on her waist and held her firmly at arm's length. It was that or kiss her, and kissing her would lead to only one thing—and that couldn't happen again until this football visit was over. But he had to equip her with a strategy to cope tonight.

'You are Princess Stella Zambrano De Santis and you will not give a damn what anyone else thinks. Tonight is nothing but a minor mission to you. You survey the room. Pick targets. Engage in brief, polite conversation. Move on to the next target. Grant them a few moments of your time.' *And then return to me.*

'Is that how *you* handle it?' she asked.

It was a skill he'd been taught. 'People are interested. I am conscious of everything I do in the public sphere. But I cannot let myself dwell on what they might *think*. It cannot be my concern.'

'I won't be a success when they find out I'm already pregnant,' she muttered. 'They'll say I trapped you. They'll say...' She trailed off.

Eduardo softened at that concern. She really didn't need to worry. 'They won't find out for a while.'

'No?' She shook her head. 'Are we going to lie and say the baby was born prematurely? Do you want me to cross my legs for an extra month or two at the end? Because, I'm sorry, that might not work.'

'Our nation has wanted a royal baby for years. They won't care about the date of its conception.' He shrugged. 'They'll be amused by my reckless passion.' Always he was the one to make the mistakes. He was the joke. But he didn't want to be a joke to *her*. He wanted to help her.

'Okay.' She looked into his eyes. Slowly he felt her straighten and square her shoulders. 'I'm sorry. I know you have more important things to do.'

He didn't want her to be sorry for sharing her concerns with him.

'Attending another opening?' He shook his head. Nothing felt more important than being with her right now.

'It's important to the people to have you there.'

'Sometimes I need a reminder too.' He grinned at her. 'I'd rather you were with me.'

It would be nice to have her at his side, sharing the intensity of the spotlight as she had that day at the restaurant. He'd catch her eye and know he wasn't alone in the crowd.

His heart thumped. 'You have everything ready otherwise? Ask Giulia for anything. Do not worry about cost. With all those royals and politicians from neighbouring countries present we need to look the part.' He sent her an apologetic look. 'And all those models and actresses—'

'Because this is your find-a-bride ball?' She looked sly.

'You heard about that?'

'How could I not? Wildfire rumours. It's like a Cinder-freaking-ella ball.'

'But instead Prince Eduardo is presenting his secret long-time love and now new wife to the world.' He gave in to temptation and kissed her quickly. 'The *scandal*.'

'You like that element, don't you?' She cupped his jaw and kept him close. 'Rebellious Prince Eduardo.'

The temptation of her was too great.

'Rebellious? I'm a married man. I've settled down and become boring.' He lifted her up and carried her to the bed.

'Never boring,' she breathed as he kissed her.

He had about four minutes. He used every second wisely.

CHAPTER THIRTEEN

JUST OVER TWELVE hours later Eduardo was struggling to breathe. For the first time in years he was anxious. Not for himself, but for her. She'd twirled for him upstairs and asked if she looked okay. He'd told her she looked beautiful. That she always did, no matter what she was wearing.

She'd told him he was a silver-tongued pirate.

Now she was only a few feet away, entrancing three diplomats. She'd been entrancing everyone in the ballroom since she'd made her grand entrance alongside him three hours ago.

Her hair had been made glossy and perfect with product and hours of the stylist's care, but he missed her workout ponytail and its hint of kink. Her make-up had been applied more heavily, to cope with the demands of the flashing bulbs of the mass-media reps, but her skin was still luminescent. Her pale pink silk dress was cut wide at the shoulder, threatening to slip should she do anything too rash with her arms. A dangerous, sexy element to such a demure-coloured dress.

Every man in the room had his eyes glued to her, hoping she'd move her arm in just the right way to send the fabric tumbling and expose those perfect plump breasts. And then there was the sapphire, resting just above those ripe treasures. There had never been such a statement as that. The jewel's significance wouldn't be lost on San Felipe society. It had been given once before to a woman who wasn't meant to be queen. To a woman who'd been adored, chosen, elevated to the throne. Breaking all the rules—putting love before duty.

So, yes, he'd chosen it deliberately, knowing that it echoed that great royal romance of a century ago. But, despite the calculation in his decision, it was perfect for her. He hadn't lied when he'd told her how it deepened her eyes.

This morning's headlines had been as he'd envisaged. She was the commoner soldier who'd stolen the Prince's heart. Tomorrow there'd be pictures of her in uniform placed alongside her 'princess makeover' look tonight. The fashion bloggers would gush over her 'transformation'. It irritated the hell out of him.

But there'd be no doubt that this was a love match. Even the innuendo-drenched pictures of them crossing the tarmac the other day emphasised that. Her popularity was assured. She'd given loyal service to her country. She was beautiful. And tonight she'd proved she could nail the glamour and grace expected of a princess.

They didn't know there was so much more to her—determination, intelligence, integrity, humour. And fragility. She'd aced her 'mission', but he wondered about the price she was going to pay.

He saw her glance at the soldiers stationed in the four corners of the room—saw the longing in her eyes. She'd rather be on the sidelines than centre stage. He understood. He felt it.

Suddenly there was nothing more important than standing with his wife, holding her hand and staring the world down. Except as he stepped towards her one of his aides requested that he meet with another of the foreign politicians in attendance.

He masked his irritation with a smile. But as he talked he kept his focus on her—and those around her. As she'd predicted, they did stare at her—all of them. Men. Women. He realised, too late, that he didn't much like it either.

There were women here who'd been tagged as possible princesses, but Antonio was too frozen to be bothered and Eduardo had stunned them all by turning up with a bride already on his arm. Part of him had enjoyed thwarting those stuffy aides' plans. But that lick of satisfaction hadn't lasted. Now he wondered how 'perfect' his plan really was—about the pressure she'd be under from here on in.

How many almost-anorexic socialites did he know?

Women who lived in the public eye were ruthlessly and relentlessly judged on their appearance, on their every move, until it almost broke them. And he'd put Stella at the epicentre of all that stress.

Eduardo's head ached. He hadn't thought this through properly. He hadn't thought about everything he was making her sacrifice and asking her to do and be. How had he ever thought this would be easy?

Hell. He hadn't *thought* at all.

He didn't want her to change, to lose herself. He didn't want her to hate this life.

But he'd put her into it. He could have let her go to New Zealand and she could have lived there in quiet, peaceful anonymity.

But he needed the child she carried. And he still wanted *her*.

Stella glanced sideways, trying to spot Eduardo. Not because she needed him, but because she wanted him to see that she was killing this moment. He was only a couple of feet away, talking to the finance minister of another small European country. As she watched Crown Prince Antonio joined him. In their formal regalia the two brothers looked so alike, but they were so different. For one thing, Eduardo was human. And so hot.

Across the small distance he met her gaze and smiled softly. Smiling back, Stella fought the instinct to put a hand to her belly. It would be the ultimate giveaway, given that her every movement was being watched and recorded, to be discussed and analysed in magazines and on daytime chat shows.

She was the news right now. She had to project the right image and protect their secret. It was the most challenging mission of her life. But she was doing okay. She even liked what she was wearing. The pleasure of success deepened her smile.

'Your Highness.'

Stella's heart seized and that smile fell as she turned to face the man who'd spoken. Her father, in full military colours, regarding her as expressionlessly as ever.

'General,' she answered quietly, aware that the people nearest them had stepped back, apparently to give them space, but at the same time avidly watching.

She waited, stupidly aching to see something in his expression. Recognition. Approval. Anger. *Anything.* But there was only the blank expression of a dutiful official. He'd stripped her of the thing she'd loved most and sent her away—alone. And now he couldn't even bring himself to speak to her.

Nothing personal. Nothing paternal. Ever.

That old disappointment leached the pleasure of success from her.

She knew there weren't just people watching, that there were cameras, but she couldn't bring herself to say anything more. She just stood silently, unable to hide her hurt.

'Stella.' Eduardo was suddenly beside her, his hand warm on her back. 'General Zambrano.'

That was when she finally saw some emotion in her father's eyes. But it wasn't the emotion she'd expected—not loyalty nor respect for the Prince. The look was utterly venomous.

She was so surprised she stepped forward. 'Father.' She reached out.

Her father glanced back at her and the bland mask dropped back into place. He didn't answer her.

'Perhaps you will visit us soon.' She faltered over her words, her father's quiet rejection slicing even deeper.

She didn't dare look at Eduardo.

He bowed again. 'I wish you well, Your Highness.' He stepped away, disappearing into the throng.

Shaken, Stella blinked, struggling to regain control and hide her hurt. She vowed once more to give her child everything she'd never had. Support. Compassion. Love.

Her victorious feeling died. Only ash was left.

Eduardo turned to her. 'Stella?'

'We'd better get mingling again.' She was aware that he was looking at her intently, but she needed to get her game face back on before she could look at him.

'Why don't we dance?' he suggested. 'They're expecting us to.'

Oh, he *had* to be kidding. 'I can't dance. I *never* dance.'

'Not at all?'

'No, and my first time isn't going to be here.'

Anger surged. She'd just been publicly rejected by her father—she wasn't about to make a fool of herself in front of the world. She might be able to wear a designer dress, but she couldn't move with the grace these glamorous women had spent their lives perfecting. She'd show them just how much of a fake—and a failure—she was.

'But it's a ball.'

'Then find another dance partner,' she snapped viciously. 'There are a million here for you to choose from. Wasn't that the point?'

She'd had enough.

He put both hands on her waist, just as she was about to push past him and stalk out. She glared up—wordlessly demanding that he let her go. But her gaze was caught—and locked—in his. His hold on her tightened.

'Are you okay?' he asked softly.

His question snuffed out her anger. All that was left was the hurt her father had inflicted. His rejection always hurt, and it never eased, but tonight's public blanking had been so much worse. And now this?

'Don't…' she whispered. His concern made her emotions impossible to control.

'Don't ask if you're okay?' His eyebrows lifted.

Desperately she tried to hold herself together. But that tender tone from him…that intensity… She couldn't bear to be exposed to anyone, but especially not to him. She ached to twist away and hide from the understanding in his eyes.

He made her too vulnerable. He made her want more than he'd ever want to give.

'Eduardo—'

'You're the only one I want to dance with,' he professed, relinquishing her waist only to take her hand in his. 'So we'll leave.'

CHAPTER FOURTEEN

THE BEST THING about a palace ball was the fact that Eduardo only had to walk up a couple of flights of stairs and a few paces down the corridor and he'd be in his own apartment, alone with his crushed wife. He wanted to smooth the stark agony from her eyes. He wanted to smash some sense into her father's skull.

In the corridor on his level, where they could still hear the music from the ballroom, he turned her to face him. She avoided his eyes—focused her fierceness on his body instead. She ran her hands up his chest, pressed her mouth to his. He understood that she wanted physical release—to feel good and forget. But staying silent and burying that hurt wasn't going to help in the long run, and he wanted to offer her more than a five-minute fix.

'No one ever taught you how to waltz?' he asked.

'I wasn't interested.' She stiffened and tried to pull away from him.

'Too busy being the tough soldier?' He firmly kept her close, despite the tension building in her body.

'Didn't find a partner,' she corrected bluntly.

'You've found one now.' Eduardo angled his head and whispered, 'Dance with me. Please.'

A flush faintly stained her pale skin. She quickly glanced up at him, awkwardness flashing. 'I'll trample on your toes.'

'I'll live.' He kept one hand on her waist and clasped her fingers, lifting her arm so they stood in formal waltz position. 'You start on the left foot, count one-two-three. It's easy.'

'You say *everything* is easy,' she muttered, looking down at their feet.

'One-two-three,' he answered, keeping time with the music wafting up the staircase.

Slowly she took the smallest of steps.

'One-two-three...' He smiled, but fell silent after a couple of bars because she already had it.

Of course she did.

He didn't speak for a long time, just let the music work its magic. Their bodies were made to move together. She was the perfect height for him in those killer heels, and he loved her lithe strength brushing against his. But more than that he loved feeling comfort creep into her. Slowly the tension receded from her body. As she relaxed he cradled her closer, so that they swayed to the graceful tune of the strings. Not really dancing, but it didn't matter. This wasn't for the look of it, but for the feel.

He'd been so preoccupied with everything these past two days he'd not thought about her father. She'd not mentioned him either. But after witnessing their interaction just then... He didn't care what the General thought of *him*, but Stella deserved so much better.

'I'm sorry,' he said finally. 'I should have arranged a meeting with your father before tonight. I should have been to see him.'

'It's not your fault. Not your responsibility.' Her lashes lifted. 'And I shouldn't have to make an appointment to see my own father.'

Her desolation haunted him. A lump blocked his throat. He didn't know what he could say to make this better for her. It was such a fundamental pain.

'I don't know why I'm surprised. Don't know why it still gets to me when it's always been the same.' She tried to smile but failed.

'He doesn't talk to you?'

'Only to give orders. He's never once told me he's proud of me. Never once said *Well done*, or *Congratulations*,' she mumbled. 'He waited more than half his life to get the wife and son he wanted. But he lost his wife. And he didn't get a son. He got me. I've always been a disappointment.'

The hurt in her voice burned. He drew her closer still, wrapping his arms around her, wanting to protect her. But the wound was already there. 'He *should* be so proud of you.'

'Nothing I've done has ever been enough.' She turned her face into his neck, hiding her eyes from him. 'He doesn't care. He never has.' Her fingers curled into his shirt. 'I won't let that happen to our baby,' she whispered rawly.

'Nor will I,' he promised.

He felt her body shake in a broken sigh. Was she crying? He bent to look into her face, but her eyes were resolutely closed.

'I'm tired,' she said.

'I know.' He lifted her into his arms.

'I can—'

'Just let me.'

He carried her into his apartment, kicking the door shut with his foot. He went straight to the dark bedroom and, still holding her close, climbed onto the bed. He carefully stroked her back, pleased when she didn't try to slip away. Instead she snuggled down, her head on his chest, her body half blanketing his.

'You have such courage, Stella,' he whispered roughly. Her strength felled him. 'He's crazy not to know how amazing you are.'

But he felt her shake her head.

'I've been so alone for so long,' she confided in a quick rush of words, as if afraid to admit it.

'You're not any more,' he promised. He was here for her. He *wanted* to be here for her. And he wanted her to lean on him. Because of him she'd have to face so many firsts. He wanted to be at her side for all of them.

He felt her release another shaky breath and she burrowed closer still. He toed off his shoes and awkwardly reached for a soft blanket to keep them both warm.

'Just sleep, sweetheart.' He took her hand and laced his

fingers through hers, his own tension ebbing as her fingers tightened on his. 'Everything is going to be okay.'

And maybe it would be.

He kissed the top of her hair and held her as close as he could. Eventually her breathing became more regular, then deepened. A wholly different kind of satisfaction thrummed in his blood. Contentment. She'd turned to him and he'd comforted her. She rested easy now, in his arms.

He wanted her to be happy. Seeing all those people clamouring for a piece of her tonight had made him think properly for the first time all week. She'd handled it beautifully, but he'd changed her life, taken so many choices from her. Hell, he'd even stopped her from running in fresh air. He wanted to fix that as best he could—he wanted to make this *work*.

When he woke they were still fully clothed in their formal ball wear, curled tightly together in that close embrace. She was still deeply asleep, and it was hours past her usual wake-up-and-train time. Her peace gave him immeasurable pleasure. But he couldn't wait until she woke. He needed to make plans.

Carefully he disentangled himself and crept out of the bedroom to shower and dress in another room.

Walking through the lounge twenty minutes later, he checked the newspapers that had been delivered. He'd been right: her approval rating was sky-high. They all thought she was beautiful. They'd captured stunning pictures of her in that soft dress and they'd caught Eduardo looking at her in a way that would leave no one in any doubt of his desire for her.

His phone buzzed.

That last picture on page one is perfection.

Matteo commenting. Matteo knowing that Eduardo would have checked today's papers already. Yeah... Because Eduardo always did his job very well.

But he didn't want their relationship to be a *job*. And now the lack of privacy rubbed at old, unhealed wounds. He didn't want the world encroaching on something that had become so personal. He needed time and space to find balance with Stella.

And to get that he was going to have to tell his iced-up brother the truth.

CHAPTER FIFTEEN

SLEEPILY STELLA REACHED out a hand, but encountered only the cool, empty sheet. She opened her eyes. Was Eduardo awake and gone already?

She checked her watch and was stunned to see she'd slept in for the first time in *years*. And she was still in her ball-gown! She rolled onto her back, bereft of his company. She should go for her run, but for once she didn't want to. She wished Eduardo was still holding her with such care. Her whole body ached with want for that. Her heart ached too. For once she'd felt treasured.

But she made herself move. She'd go for a swim. Water always eased raw wounds.

She stripped out of her dress, pulled on a swimsuit and robe, then stole down the stairs to get to the ground level. As she darted along the rose-covered walkway towards the poolhouse she saw the two brothers standing near the tennis court gate. And as she stepped closer, she could hear, because their voices were rising in volume.

'This was the best—'

'You should have told me beforehand,' Antonio interrupted Eduardo, icily furious.

'This is the *heir*, Antonio. Don't you see that?' he snapped back.

Stella knew she shouldn't stay and listen. She should turn and walk away before they saw her. Or step forward so they *did* see her. But she couldn't. She stayed right where she was, hidden by foliage.

'What I see is that you're a bigger fool than I thought possible.'

Stella realised Eduardo had just told his brother about the

baby—and now the Crown Prince was more disapproving than ever. As she'd known he would be.

'I'm not the impetuous idiot I once was. From every angle this was the best solution,' Eduardo answered back. 'You know I'm right.'

'This is *not* what I wanted for you,' Antonio said harshly, his voice an icy whip.

'She's exactly what we need her to be.' Eduardo now sounded as ice-cold as his brother. 'Haven't you seen the papers? After that wedding picture was leaked Matteo planted the few details necessary for her to be a hit. After last night's performance her success is snowballing. She's just what San Felipe needs. I can control this, Antonio.'

'Can you control *her*?'

'Of course.'

Stella closed her eyes at Eduardo's arrogance and his cold, businesslike assumption. After he'd been so tender last night. This *hurt*. This hurt so much more than anything.

'So this is not a love match?' Antonio said bluntly.

Stella's world stopped in that moment of silence before Eduardo answered. And then her husband was as brutally blunt as his brother.

'What prince has ever married for love?'

Humiliation burned a hole in her heart. Swiftly she turned, sprinting back inside. She'd known she shouldn't have listened. She'd known this was an orchestrated marriage of convenience. But to know that Eduardo wanted his child to become the *Crown Prince*, even when he saw his brother suffer under the weight of the role, even when he railed against the constraints on himself...

She didn't want those pressures and limitations and 'controls' for her child. She didn't want the lack of choice. She didn't want the lack of love.

And she didn't want it for *herself*. She wanted what she'd had a taste of last night—tenderness, caring, someone to be there for her. But it had been a charade—part of his Prince

Charming act. It had only been to control the situation, to control *her* and create a successful 'story' for the royal family—more San Felipe myth.

She'd thought she was no longer alone. She'd been so wrong. She'd never been as alone as she was now. And it had never hurt so much.

Eduardo realised his mistake as soon as he'd made the facetious reply. He'd been trying to play it as emotionlessly as Antonio. But he'd forgotten.

'I'm sorry,' he muttered.

It was too late. His brother had disappeared beneath an even thicker layer of ice. Eduardo hadn't been able to break through it in a decade. He didn't think anyone would.

Antonio had vowed to devote his life to duty when Alessia died and he was cemented in it now. Eduardo had made a vow too—to help his brother however he could. To try and make amends. To try and share some of his burden. Because he remembered the old days, when his brother had teased him, telling him his hair was too long or his jokes too lame. When they'd laughed together. He hadn't heard Antonio laugh in so long.

'*I* would have married for love.' Antonio's voice like the thinnest, sharpest shard of ice.

It was the rarest hint of emotion.

'I know.' Eduardo bent his head. He'd caused hurt twice over. 'Stella needs to go back to Secreto Real, Antonio. She needs time to rest and adjust. I'm sorry.'

Sorry for so much more than wanting some time out.

'Then cancel your engagements and stay with her. Not even *you* can be seen to discard your new bride so quickly.' Displeasure flared in his eyes.

Eduardo burned inside but took the hit silently. He had no intention of ditching Stella.

'But not until after the opening night at the opera tonight,' Antonio added. 'Salvatore Accardi is going to be there, and I need you to maintain cordial relations seeing as neither of us are going to marry his precious daughter.' Antonio looked bitter as he mentioned the notoriously corrupt nobleman both brothers preferred to avoid. 'Then you can go.'

'Fine.' All Eduardo wanted was to be back on the little island with Stella, with the time to build on the fragile foundations forming between them.

Leaving Antonio, he walked towards his apartment, wondering if Sleeping Beauty had woken. His phone buzzed. He paused in the middle of the corridor when he saw the contact's name on the screen.

He answered swiftly. 'Dr Russo? Is anything wrong?'

'No, I just wanted to let you know I've secured a specialist to see Stella early next week. As you know, I've tried to alleviate her concerns, but she's still apprehensive, of course. I read her mother's file at the hospital and the haemorrhage she had didn't stem from an inheritable condition. Also, Stella is much younger than her mother was—fitter and stronger too. I think seeing the specialist will reassure her. We'll set up more frequent appointments from there.'

Eduardo stood rooted to the spot, utterly shocked as the doctor continued.

'She will have a full scan at that appointment too. I know she enjoyed listening to the baby's heartbeat on Friday.'

Stella had heard the baby's heartbeat? She'd seen the doctor and not told him? And what the *hell* had happened to her mother?

Eduardo forced himself to answer. 'Indeed. Thank you for your discretion in coming to me directly. Come to me always where her health is concerned.' He wanted to know every damn thing. And he was furious *she* hadn't told him.

'Of course, Your Highness.'

He ended the call and just stared at his phone for a second. Then he veered away from his private apartment to his office on the intermediary floor. He grabbed Stella's personnel file, seething with self-directed anger for not reading it closely enough. But he'd skipped those bare facts detailing her parents—he'd wanted to get the facts about *her*. Now he stopped to check that earlier information.

Stella had been born just before midnight on April the twenty-third. Her mother had died on April the twenty-fourth, a mere two hours later.

Her mother had died because of complications on delivering her daughter. Was that why her father was so hard on her—because he'd never forgiven her?

Why hadn't she told him this last night—he'd thought that she was opening up to him. That he'd helped her in some way. But she hadn't shared even half of her battle. She hadn't spoken with him about seeing Dr Russo two days ago. About being scared. About having any kind of scan.

Stella was the epitome of health and strength. She hadn't even had any morning sickness. Now he remembered that look in her eyes when they'd watched the pregnancy test result. She'd looked terrified. She still was terrified. Of the birth.

But she hadn't told him. She'd shut him out. And then she'd heard their child's heart beating without him.

Rejection dug deep, bitter poison in its claws. He'd thought they had a chance. But she'd kept something vital a secret. She hadn't turned to him. She hadn't trusted him.

He went back down the corridor and up the stairs to his apartment. Of course she was awake. Of course she was in her trainers, running pants and a grey tee shirt.

He breathed in, trying to stay in control.

'You're going on the treadmill?' he asked.

She nodded and stepped onto the machine.

'Is all this exercise what's best for the baby?' He tested her—would she talk?

'You said this marriage was what's *best* for the baby.' Stella started jogging. 'But you plan for this baby to be the next Crown Prince or Princess of San Felipe.'

His focus sharpened. She wouldn't look at him and was obviously angry—was she sorry she'd talked to him last night? Did she regret opening up to him even that little bit?

'Right?' she prompted him. 'So this baby will have a life of even greater restriction than your own?'

She was back to this again. Pushing for a way out instead of telling him what she was really scared of. Pushing *him* away.

'You've known all along that this is a royal child,' he challenged her. 'The possibility of the crown has always been there.'

'But you've *planned* it.'

'I hardly planned for you to get pregnant,' he said. Her bitterness multiplied his.

'But you've orchestrated *everything* since you found out.'

'Because I've had to.' And she appreciated *none* of his efforts. She didn't want anything he had to offer. She didn't trust him at all.

Stella glanced over and saw Eduardo's expression close down. How could he go so quickly from caring to completely cold-hearted? It scared her. She couldn't trust in those precious moments of last night because now he gave her that damn silent, 'dare you to talk first' treatment. And that made her anger incandescent.

'Is there some ancient decree that whichever of you has the first child then she or he gets the crown?' she asked. 'Is this some kind of sibling jealousy and you're determined that the lineage will continue from the seed of *your* loins because you can't be the one thing you want so very badly?'

She was spouting rubbish now, just aiming to get a reaction other than ice—she didn't care how.

Now that fire in his eyes kindled—but it wasn't passion. 'Says you, the woman who's spent all her life trying to be the one thing she can't be—'

'I am an exceptional soldier.'

'But you can't be the son your father wanted.'

She recoiled, jumping off that damn treadmill.

'You can't even please him,' he added.

'Yet you want to do that same thing to your own child,'

she pointed out to him angrily. 'To place all those unwanted expectations on a baby.'

'This is different.'

'No, it's not.' She shook her head. 'You set *everything* up. It's like a slickly edited tourism video. The photos. That sapphire, with that whole legend around it. Releasing my service record. All fodder for the press.'

'We need the public to believe in you. In us.'

And he'd gotten them to. He'd also made *her* believe—in herself and in the possibility of *them*. He'd known which buttons to push, how to pull her in, because she was so starved of attention and so stupid. He'd been so suave and convincing and she'd fallen in *love* with him. It had just been a couple of steps from crush to complete adoration. But the tenderness she'd thought he felt for her had been a façade. He was as frozen and as duty-filled as his brother.

'And that's all that matters to you, isn't it?' She realised now the extent of his emptiness. 'You're never going to open up to me,' she said slowly. To think she'd thought he could love her... No one loved her. And it *hurt*. 'You can't let anyone in. Not your brother. Not a woman. No one.' She blinked to hold back the stinging tears.

But something had changed in his eyes. He was still watching her intently, but the fire had died. Something cold had taken its place. 'Maybe the pregnancy hormones are finally getting to you.'

'No, they're not.' She wasn't letting him pin this on her hormones.

That was when she recognised his expression—it was *disapproval*.

'Maybe you're tired.'

'Tired of this, yes.' She was *so* tired of not being what anyone wanted.

'Then I'll see you later, when you've had a chance to rest.' He walked away from her.

'Seriously? You're leaving?'

'I have business I must attend to,' he said. He was no

suave, joking prince now. His eyes were almost as dead as Antonio's.

'Business that's more important than this?' More important than *her*?

'You're tired, Stella.'

'And you can't cope with any emotion, can you? Other than sexual hunger,' she called after him, satisfied when he turned back to face her. 'What are you going to do when your child is crying—walk away then too?' He turned away again, but she stalked after him. 'You're as closed-up as your brother. You can't trust and you can't love,' she said, her voice husky and breaking as he got to the door. 'I'm not staying here.'

'What do you think you're going to do?' he taunted softly. 'Walk out through the front door? It doesn't work like that, Stella.'

'I'll *make* it,' she promised angrily. 'Because I won't let my child grow up with such an emotionally stunted father. You think you can give this child riches, but you're poor in what really matters. I won't let my child grow up in an atmosphere devoid of love.'

'Then *you* love it, Stella. That's why you're here,' he said bluntly. 'Because *I* have to do my duty.'

'Of course you do,' she said bleakly, feeling the blow to her heart. 'And I have to do *my* duty—to my baby.'

CHAPTER SIXTEEN

STELLA GRIPPED THE back of a chair as Eduardo slammed the door behind him. Leaving her. He didn't think for a minute that she'd escape. And he was right. How could she, with all the royal protection officers, the cameras, the security here keeping people out? Keeping her trapped.

Then you *love it. That's why you're here.*

He couldn't have been clearer. He wasn't going to be the father she needed for her child. And she knew how much it hurt to have a parent who let you down time and time again. To have a husband who was just as emotionally unavailable and unsupportive... That would tear her in two.

He'd been so cold. A different person from the man who'd held her, listened to her, cared for her last night. For an hour she'd felt that heaven might be right here. But he'd ripped that façade away in seconds this morning.

She crumpled to the floor, tears running down her face.

'Stella?'

She looked up as the door opened again. Then she groaned and lifted her hands to hide her face. *Her father was here.* He'd finally turned up and it was when she least wanted to see him.

'Stella?' He rushed towards her. 'What's happened?'

'Nothing.' She quickly stood up and stepped back. As if she could ever tell *him.*

But the tears wouldn't stop. And she couldn't breathe properly.

'I'm sorry you have to see me like this. Crying like a... *girl.*' She sniffed. So angry and hurt and humiliated. 'Can we talk later?'

'No.' Her father had stopped a foot from her, his face ashen. 'This can't wait.'

She pulled a handful of tissues from a box on the desk and drew in another deep breath. But she couldn't control the sobs.

'Stop, Stella.' Her father reached out and touched her shoulder.

She froze, waited for what felt like eons before he spoke again, gravelly, sombre and slow.

'When I saw you last night at the ball with him I wondered. Thought maybe I'd been wrong. But it seems I wasn't.'

'Wrong about what?' What was her uncommunicative father trying to tell her?

He sat down heavily in a nearby chair and looked up at her. 'A few months ago you went missing from the barracks for the afternoon,' he said slowly, looking more tired than she'd ever seen him. 'That same day Prince Eduardo pulled out of a public appearance at the last minute. He was due to speak at a gallery not far from the base. When he was seen the next day he had a black eye. He made lame jokes about falling over but there was conjecture—it was the kind of bruise you got from a fight, not a crash into a door.'

General Zambrano stopped. The grim look became a thunderous frown again.

'The next thing you're pregnant, and clearly shocked about it. Then you disappear—only to reappear a few days later *married* to the Prince.'

Stella stared at her father. That was the longest speech he'd given her in years. 'What are you asking me?'

'Did he hurt you? Did you try to fight him off and fail?'

Her father thought Eduardo had assaulted her in some way?

'Oh, no. No. No. *No.*' Stella stepped closer, so shocked her tears stopped. 'Eduardo would *never*...'

Her father didn't look relieved. 'I wouldn't let him serve in the army because of the risk to other soldiers. He would have been a target. He can serve the country better elsewhere and Prince Antonio agrees. But Eduardo was very angry.'

'He still is.' Stella managed half a smile. 'He would have been a good soldier.'

'Did he hurt you?' her father asked again.

'Not in the way you mean. *Never.*' She looked down, embarrassed at discussing something so personal with her father. 'What we've shared, I've wanted. The trouble is I want more than he's able to give me.'

'Meaning?'

'Meaning we had a very brief affair and I got pregnant and he's done "the right thing"... More than that, he's done everything he can to protect me and this baby. But that's all it is.'

'Is he supportive?' Her father cleared his throat. 'He's ensuring you have the best doctors?'

'Of course.' Her heart seized. She still hadn't told Eduardo. She *couldn't*—certainly not now. But because of her position as his wife she'd have the best specialist care.

'You were arguing. I heard raised voices from along the corridor. And you're upset.'

'Because I've been stupid.' To her horror, her eyes filled with tears again.

'Stella...'

She couldn't stand such a quiet word from her father. From the *General*.

'I can't be with a man who doesn't love me,' she cried. 'I won't live like that any more. I deserve more.' She covered her face with her hands, willing her father to leave.

But he didn't move.

'I've tried to protect you for so long,' he said unevenly. 'Misguidedly.'

She looked up at him. He thought he'd been *protecting* her? 'You wouldn't let them promote me.'

In his eyes she saw so much. Hopelessness. Helplessness. Vulnerability. *Love.*

Her heart broke all over again.

'What can I do?' he asked gruffly.

'I need to get away from here,' she said wretchedly. 'I need time to think.'

He stood. 'How quickly can you be ready?'

'I'm a soldier. I'm ready now.'

'Then I'll arrange it.'

Wordless, she felt her eyes well up again. All she could do was nod and turn away.

He would never open up to her the way she'd like him to. Never give her a paternal hug. Never tell her he loved her. But finally it seemed he might try to show her.

CHAPTER SEVENTEEN

EDUARDO STALKED ALONG the long corridor back to his apartment. Five hours had passed since their argument and his anger hadn't lessened any.

She was scared about her pregnancy. That was why she'd called for Dr Russo. She hadn't wanted to tell *him*—her husband. She didn't trust him. Didn't want to confide in him. Didn't want to be with him. She'd said he was emotionally stunted.

He was feeling *all* the emotions now.

'Stella?' he called, as soon as he opened his apartment door. But his voice rang out unanswered in the empty atmosphere.

Adrenalin hit, bunching muscles, sharpening focus. Swiftly he sought out her belongings, but her duffel was missing, along with her old jeans and tee shirts and her trainers. She'd left her rings on the table beside the bed. Midnight's Passion was beside them, the platinum chain coiled around it.

Shocked, he released the breath he hadn't realised he'd been holding.

She'd left him. She'd walked out through the front door. Of course she had. Because she was a damn good soldier, always a survivor, and she'd escaped.

From *him*.

His breathing quickened, lungs hurting. *Heart* hurting. He bent his head, screwing up his eyes so the sight of the sapphire wouldn't mock him.

But it still did. God, it hurt. He wanted her. Needed her back. He *loved* her.

He swore. Short, pithy, pained. Then he moved. He had to freaking well move. He had to *find* her.

He picked up his phone. Called a captain he trusted.

'The Princess. When did you last see her?' he demanded, the second the guy answered.

'Uh, the General came to see her and—'

'When was that?' Eduardo scowled, sourness sinking into his gut.

'He arrived just before you left for the hospital,' the Captain answered warily.

After Eduardo had argued with her and walked out. Had she had a showdown with her father? 'When did the General leave?'

'I believe they went out to lunch—'

'They *what*?' Confounded, Eduardo couldn't believe his ears.

'Uh...lunch. At a restaurant, I think—'

Eduardo didn't bother listening to the rest. He turned on his heel and ran to the other end of the palace to General Carlos Zambrano's quarters. He thudded on the door so hard it rattled the hinges. And sure enough General Carlos himself answered it.

'Where is Stella?' He pushed past the man into the room.

'She's your wife. Shouldn't you know?'

'She is her own person,' Eduardo clipped an answer as he looked around the lounge. 'You really had lunch with her?'

'No, I've been in a meeting,' the General answered.

The old man was lying. Eduardo should have come back to the palace hours ago. But he'd been unable to cancel that last engagement because he hadn't wanted to let them down at the last minute. Instead he'd let Stella down.

'My daughter is very strong,' the General said. 'She doesn't grant many people the power to hurt her.' He looked at him very carefully, his frown deepening. 'I thought *you* had hurt her.'

'I have.'

'No.' Carlos moved impatiently. 'I mean physically. Back when she got pregnant.'

Dumbfounded, Eduardo stared, and then rage seared. 'I would *never*—'

'That's what she told me.' Her father raised his hands. 'She said you are a good man. I was just…protective. And unwilling to trust her judgement.'

'Good Lord, you *really* give her a hard time.' Eduardo breathed hard to recover his equilibrium. He was *furious*. What had he ever done to make him think that? He might be arrogant and entitled, but he wasn't a psychopath.

'I'm sorry.' The General sighed. 'No man was ever going to be good enough for her. Not even a prince.'

Eduardo stared at the older man, seeing for the first time the pallor, the anxiety in his eyes. 'What the hell is going on?'

'I'm worried about her,' Carlos admitted gruffly. 'I lost her mother and it all but destroyed me. All these years I did what I thought was best for Stella. But I think I have been wrong. In sending her away…in protecting her from active duty—'

'In helping her run away from me. That was wrong.' Eduardo struggled to stay calm.

The General froze.

'I know you've helped her.' Eduardo's anger simmered like a pot of molten lava, yet he was still unable to believe this horrible reality. 'You might as well tell me where she is now, because I will find her. I have more resources, more patience than you can imagine. I *have* to know she is okay. I have to see that for myself.'

He realised now just how fragile she was. And just how courageous.

Last night he'd told her she wasn't alone any more. But the first time she'd questioned it—the first time she'd needed him—he'd walked out. She'd been hurt and he'd hurt her more. Because he'd been so wrapped up in his own insecurity he hadn't seen how truly upset she'd been.

He was an idiot. She'd *never* had the emotional security she'd craved. Of *course* she was going to test him. This morning she'd done what she did best and challenged him. And he'd let her down.

He shouldn't have left her to wake by herself, because

something had happened to set off her doubts. He shouldn't have stood there silently judging her when she still hadn't told him her fears about the birth. These were *huge* fears for her, and she'd needed to feel totally safe before she shared them. He'd needed to *earn* that trust. And now she'd run away because she was used to being alone. Because she thought she still was.

That broke his heart.

How could he expect her to open up to him the way he wanted when he hadn't done the same? He'd shut her out from how he really felt. So often when they'd verged on true intimacy he'd turned things physical. Kept her close, but kept that last bit of himself distant. Safe. Until last night.

Those kids he'd seen at the hospital today kept on fighting. They faced things far more fearful. He'd been a coward. After that day on the beach he'd been too proud to chase her—in reality he'd been too much of a chicken. Because he'd been as freaked out by the intensity of that afternoon as she had. Only he hadn't been man enough to admit it—not even to himself.

Then fate had given him a second chance, and he'd gladly taken advantage of it.

Yet he'd still screwed it up.

So he'd damn well find her. But as soon as he knew she was okay he'd set her free. If she still wanted to, she could live overseas. He'd find her a safe haven. His heart tore at the thought of letting her go, but he'd do whatever was necessary to ensure her happiness.

'You all right? You're breathing funny.'

The General was staring at him as if he'd grown an extra head.

'I need to find her.'

'You should already know where she is,' her father said. 'She's where she always goes when she needs time to think.'

She wanted to think? Hope bubbled up within him. If she needed to *think* then it might not be too late.

Now *he* tried to think. Stella's answer to everything was exercise. She always went for a run. Or a swim.

The answer hit like a lightning bolt and he almost laughed at the simplicity. The obviousness. More hope bubbled. He didn't deserve her if he wasn't right. If he took the Maserati he could get there in less than half an hour...

But his way out of the palace was blocked by his brother, standing in the high-studded, gilded atrium, clad in an Armani tuxedo and adjusting a gleaming cufflink.

'Are you ready?' Antonio scowled at Eduardo's jeans.

He'd forgotten about the opening night of the freaking opera and the damn politicians he was supposed to schmooze. 'Antonio, I can't right now.'

His brother looked implacable. 'All I need you to do is—'

'I can't go with you.' Eduardo interrupted shortly.

His brother's expressionless eyes narrowed. 'What's wrong?'

'It's Stella. She's gone.'

'Already?'

'Be human!' Eduardo shouted. 'Be human for one goddamn minute.'

Antonio stood so rigid he looked as if he'd been cast in metal.

'I'm *sorry* that you lost Alessia.' Eduardo gazed at his brother and offered his wretched apology. 'I am *so* sorry I never told you she was sick. I will *always* be sorry that I never told you.'

His lungs hurt with the effort of breathing. With the effort of not pushing past Antonio and combing the streets in a desperate, hopeless, fear-filled search.

'I know you put the Crown first. But I'm not you. I can't do that. Stella comes first for me now and she always will. I can't be here. I can't do this. I have to go after her.'

As he went to go past him Antonio gripped his arm with a vice-like hand. Eduardo turned and looked into his brother's face. They almost stood eye to eye.

'I don't blame you for my not going to see Alessia sooner.'

Antonio spoke with quiet, lethal intensity. 'I could have gone. So many times. And I didn't. That was my decision. My fault. My guilt.'

Eduardo shook his head. 'I should have told you. I should have made you go. I should have been a better brother. To you and to her.'

A muscle jerked in Antonio's jaw. But then he lifted his hand and ruffled Eduardo's hair in that old tease of years ago. 'It's still too long, but it suits you.' He released Eduardo with a small, wry smile. 'Go. Get out of here. Do what's right.'

Eduardo heard Antonio's quiet words behind him as he strode away.

'Do what I didn't.'

CHAPTER EIGHTEEN

THE TIDE HAD TURNED. Waves rushed higher. In another hour there'd only be a narrow strip of dry sand left at the base of the cliff. She needed to walk back around the rocks to the bay. She wasn't going to risk free-climbing up the cliff now she had a baby on board.

She splashed in the water, her sandals wet. Her father's man was waiting around the next bay, ready to drive her wherever she wanted to go. She just had to decide where that was going to be.

To Eduardo? Or to anonymity on an island a thousand miles away from this one?

She knew where he'd gone. Her father had told her. And even though it was for a good cause it had made her angrier. She'd have gone with him if he'd asked her to. If he'd told her. But he hadn't asked. And she hadn't said anything either. She hadn't told him so much. Neither of them had.

That was when it finally hit her. Everything that was wrong with her father was also wrong with *her*. She'd been so uncommunicative it was unfair.

She could create a good life for herself here. She could be brave. She could tell Eduardo she'd fallen for him and ask him to be gentle when he wanted out of their marriage. It wasn't his fault he didn't love her. He desired her. He respected her. Couldn't that be enough to make this a success?

Not if she kept acting like a sulky, spoilt child.

She'd spent her life trying to please her father, instead of letting it go and just being herself. Pleasing herself. Her life could have been so much richer if she hadn't tried to control herself and remained so intensely focused on that one goal. She'd been without friends and lonely for so long because she hadn't let people in. She could have *joked* with some of her fellow soldiers about the General being her dad. Instead she'd isolated herself by trying to prove herself for so long.

Eduardo was lonely and isolated too. Mired in that conflict between duty and desire. As Giulia had said, they had much in common.

So maybe they could be more than husband and wife. Maybe they could be a team. They could achieve a whole bunch of stuff together.

Finally she admitted the truth to herself—the hurt and anger she felt wasn't about the baby. It had *never* been about the baby. Her fears had been for herself. She'd been in lust with him from the start, but once she'd got to know him she'd fallen hard, and it hurt to know he didn't feel the same. But she had to grow up—she was stronger than this. She had to go back.

She turned, walking ankle-deep into the water again to walk around the bay. But she'd taken only a few paces when she saw him splashing towards her. His jeans were half soaked, his hair a tousled mess, but he looked magnificent. Fiery, full of energy, he almost crackled as he moved. He strode towards her, his arms lifting as if he was about to pull her hard against him. Only he checked himself, lowering his hands and shoving them into his pockets. He opened his mouth, but then blew out a deep breath rather than saying anything.

'Did he tell you where I was?' she asked.

'No. He didn't let you down.' He looked at her sodden sandals and the wet half of her skirt. 'You've been swimming?'

She shook her head. 'The rip is too strong, I wouldn't want to get carried away.'

He nodded, his eyes hollowed and burning. 'Are you okay?'

'Why are you here?' Her heart stalled while she waited for his answer.

'I'm sorry you have to ask that.' He splashed closer. 'I'm so sorry, Stella.'

Her heart pounded, pushing hope in small pulses around

her body. 'My father told me where you went this afternoon. Your private schedule. The hospital. He said you call
in there all the time. That you know some of the kids really
well.' Her voice faded.

'Don't go thinking I'm any kind of hero,' he said. 'I only
do it because it makes me feel good.'

'Because you like them fawning over you? It's some ego
trip?'

He pressed his lips together again. She knew he wasn't
going to defend himself against the stupid suggestion. And
that was so typical of him.

'I know it's not that,' she said softly. 'I think it's because
you like to see them smile.'

He liked to see lots of people smile. He was kind that way.

'It's nothing, Stella,' he muttered.

'It's *not* nothing.' She hated it that he belittled what he
did. That he didn't believe in himself. What he did *mattered*
to so many.

For a second he looked so vulnerable it broke her heart
all over again.

'You mostly spend time with the young adults. The ones
like Alessia,' she added. 'That can't be easy for you.'

'It's—'

'Don't say it's nothing again, or I'll have to hurt you.'

A smile glimmered in his eyes, then it faded. 'I can't ever
make it right.'

Was he always going to punish himself for that? 'You
were young, and it wasn't a fair secret you'd been asked to
keep.'

'There's no excuse. I shouldn't have told my girlfriend.'

'You should have been able to trust her. It's good to be
able to talk to the people you love. To share your burdens…
She was in the wrong. Not you.'

And he'd been paying for that mistake ever since. That
was why he did everything his brother asked of him. Why he
didn't push for more freedom. He didn't think he deserved
it. He felt he owed.

'He is the loneliest person, and there is so little I can do to help him.' Eduardo lifted his head and looked directly into her eyes. 'Why did you leave? You want to leave San Felipe for good?'

'Not San Felipe.' She gazed up at him, her heart melting, and yet now the moment was here she was more scared than ever in her life before.

'Me,' he said heavily. 'You don't want the baby to end up like me.'

'No...' she whispered, shocked that he'd ever think that. 'I thought I needed—'

'You need—' Eduardo interrupted, then pulled up short. For a second that old arrogance flashed over his face. But then it faded. 'I don't want to fight this any more, Stella. I surrender.'

She stared for a moment. 'Surrender what?' She suddenly lost the battle to contain her emotions. 'Our marriage? What you want for the baby?' Had he given up on her already?

'No. Neither of those things. Or both of them, if that's what you want.' He stopped and shrugged. 'The decision is yours, Stella. Our future is in your hands.'

'What?' The faintest whisper.

His hands gripped her cold ones. 'I was so angry when I found out you were pregnant. Because you hadn't *told* me. You hadn't come to me. You were just going to walk away and not let me have any kind of say—'

'I hadn't even had a chance to think about what I was going to do,' she interrupted.

'I know that now, but back then I'd made my plan and I thought it was perfect. I thought I could control what was between us—lust. Controllable. Finite. It always has been before. And I thought I could control *you*. The palace officials wanted either Antonio or me to marry—but it was always going to be me. This way I got to present them with a *fait accompli* before they started parading prospective brides in front of me. *My* woman, with an heir already on the way and an end in sight when we'd had enough. I thought I'd risen above that anger and turned the situation to my advantage. The perfect solution.'

He squeezed her hands gently.

'But I hadn't thought through the impact of any of it on you. I hadn't thought about your needs at all. I was so arrogant. What woman wouldn't want to be my Princess, right? What an honour...what an amazing lifestyle... And a fat pay-off waiting for her at the end as long as she kept quiet and obedient. I thought I was doing you the biggest favour and that you should be grateful.' He grimaced. 'I was an asshole. I'm sorry.'

'I *did* want to be your Princess,' she said quietly. 'I liked it.'

'But it's not what you wanted.' He looked down. '*I'm* not what you wanted.'

'I slept with you within ten seconds of meeting you,' she reminded him with a wry smile. 'How can you say you're not what I wanted?'

His lips twisted, but it was a sad-edged smile. 'Lust.'

'*Uncontrollable,*' she whispered bravely. '*Infinite.*'

'Stella—' He lifted one hand to cup her jaw.

'It was a good plan.' She overrode him, speaking quickly, because she needed to have her say before he said something that would stop her. She feared his pity more than anything. 'In some ways it was the only possible plan.'

'But you left.'

Again. Now she knew she'd hurt him. And if she had the power to hurt him that was because he cared. Hope, and a cautious confidence, began to flow.

'You were right. Your title can give this baby so much— how could I deny it all those benefits? Those rights? And you were right in saying that I could give the child love...but I'd always lacked love. Or I thought I had. And that was the real problem. So the truth...?' She swallowed. 'This pregnancy was my excuse for running. All this time I was deluding my- self that all that mattered was the baby...that I was putting the baby first… Really it was all about *me*. I left because I was a coward. I couldn't bear to be with you—'

'You are *afraid* of me?' He actually lost colour.

'I'm afraid of wanting what I didn't think you could give me, nor wanted to give me.' Her confidence slipped as she saw the storm clouds gathering in his eyes. 'I heard you talking to Antonio. *"What prince ever marries for love?"'*

'Stella—'

'Let me speak—please let me speak,' she interrupted him again, twisting her hands free of his and holding them up to stop him. 'I've not spoken up the way I should and I have to now.'

She sighed as she saw him grit his teeth, and her eyes watered dangerously. She cleared her throat. She couldn't let emotion get in the way—not now.

'I thought I didn't want to spend the rest of my life trying to earn the love and approval of someone who'd become everything to me. Not all over again.' She drew another tight-chested breath. 'But then I realised that it doesn't matter. Because when you love someone you do everything you can for them.'

As she spoke, her heart felt as if it was growing, about to burst, but with each word her voice weakened.

'And one of the most important things is to talk to them.' She tried to smile, but it was hard to speak honestly about something so personal. She'd never felt so vulnerable. 'That's where I'm not so good. In fact I'm as bad as my dad. All action, not enough words. Never the words.'

Silence fell and she looked up at him. Her pirate prince was utterly still now, but he was nothing like a stone statue. He was too vibrant, too vital, too hot. She could hardly bear to look at him, but she couldn't turn away. She couldn't give up on this. On him. On *them*.

'What are the words, Stella?' he prompted her, more gentle than she'd ever heard him.

Her throat and chest were so tight they ached, and while she ought to be deafened by the thundering pace of her heart beating, all she could hear was the strained silence that she couldn't seem to breach. Finally, right on the edge, she'd lost the nerve to step off and make the leap.

'How could I admit to Antonio what I could hardly admit to myself?' Eduardo said softly, after another unbearable, seemingly endless second. 'I thought it would burn itself out, but it only burns hotter. That crazy moment on this beach was merely the spark that lit a fire that's fuelled by much more than lust.'

He paused, his frown deepening.

'Why didn't you tell me you needed to see Dr Russo?' The blue of his eyes was almost black. 'Why didn't you tell me you were worried? He called me after I'd seen Antonio this morning. I was angry you hadn't told me... I thought we'd gotten so close last night... But then to find out you'd held back something so important... That you wouldn't turn to me...'

She opened her mouth, but nothing came out. She'd frozen at the hurt she saw in him.

'I hate being excluded,' he said rawly. 'When the people I care about don't tell me what they're going through it makes me feel...feel like I can't help them. Feel that they think what I have to offer isn't enough...'

She *had* hurt him. And that was why he'd shut her out this morning. He'd been as hurt as she. Neither of them able to articulate their true fears. Both of them scared of trusting.

But there had to be that leap now.

'It's just that I was scared,' she mumbled, desperate to explain. 'Not of you,' she clarified quickly. 'I'm a soldier. I'm supposed to be brave. But I'm terrified about giving birth.'

'Oh, sweetheart.'

'And I was scared you only cared about the baby. Not really me. And I didn't want to bother you.' She closed her eyes. 'I hate being so pathetic.'

He placed his hands on her waist, firmly anchoring her. 'The last thing you are is pathetic. You don't have to be alone

and scared. You don't have to be either of those things ever
again.'

Her tears spilled from beneath the closed lashes. And despite that massive lump in her throat she could finally speak
clearly. 'I had this huge crush on you for so long, and then
all this happened and I just wanted *more*. *You* were so much
more than I'd ever imagined. So charming, so sexy...and then
so funny and kind. So much more a prince than I'd thought...
And then I didn't want to be the bride you bedded, who had
your baby and who you then walked away from. I wanted
the whole fairy tale. And it wasn't fair of me. It wasn't real-
istic of me to expect everything from you—'

'Why not?' he interrupted. 'I want more from *you*. I want
everything from you.'

He enfolded her in warmth and strength. She melted into
his arms, reaching up to kiss him. A kiss full of desperation
and apology and desire. And so much love.

He broke away with a pained groan. 'We need to tell your
father you're okay. He's worried.'

'Maybe we could invite him to have lunch soon?'

She was so happy, so full of future possibilities, she saw
now that she needed to try again. Her father had offered to
help. Maybe, with Eduardo's support, she could open up to
him too—maybe they could rebuild a relationship outside
of regimental duty.

'He'll have to come in the helicopter. We're going back
to Secreto Real for the next few weeks.' Eduardo brushed
her hair back with gentle fingers.

'We are?'

'If that's okay with you.' He gazed into her eyes for a moment, then rested his forehead on hers as if he couldn't bear
to stand more than an inch away from her. 'We need time,
Stella,' he said softly. 'Fortunately we have for ever.'

She lifted her chin and met his kiss. Tender and true and
so emotional. She clung to him .

'I love you,' he said.

Two fat tears trickled down her face. He kissed them

away, but the lump in her throat grew. She knew she had to push past it.

'No one...' she whispered, but her voice gave out.

'No one what?'

She could see him thinking.

His eyes widened and he asked in a strangled voice. 'You've never heard that before?'

She couldn't even shake her head, her throat was so tight, and for a split-second she wanted to look away from him, to hide safely behind her personal ramparts. But it was too late. And, as exposed as she was, she was glad it was him seeing her now.

'Oh, Stella.' His expression softened, but the embrace he enveloped her in was fierce. 'Not even your father?' He ran his hands up her back. 'I love you, I love you, I love you.'

He kissed her, *held* her. She leaned as close as she could. She never wanted to leave his arms.

He scooped her up and with keen determination quickly looked about. After three strides he turned and sank onto the sand at the very base of the cliff. His arms loosened enough for her to wriggle and wrap her legs around his waist. Embracing him. She kissed him back, pouring herself into the passion, wanting to give him everything she could. She'd missed him, needed him. She couldn't get close enough.

'I was worried I'd lost you,' he groaned breathlessly, between kisses that grew both frantic and yet more tender. 'That I was never going to have you...not *really* have you. Not like this.'

She took the lead, impatient and yet aching to savour the preciousness of this moment. She grappled with the zipper of his jeans. He shifted beneath her, helping. Helping again by sliding his hand under her skirt, up her thighs, pulling her panties aside enough to access her secret heat. But then she hesitated, looking deeply into his eyes, drawing courage from what she saw in them. Her heart soared. Lust was a mere fraction of all she was feeling.

'I love you,' she whispered.

There was another flawless moment of silent, straining emotion before he breathed—a broken sigh of pleasure, an aching heart filled to bursting.

'Another first?' he whispered back, gazing into her eyes as she nodded. 'The most precious,' he muttered gruffly.

Her eyes remained locked with his as she sank down, taking him hard and deep within. Her core moulded around his, strengthening, securing. They both sighed at the searing sweetness. Fully clothed, yet bared to the soul, Stella had never felt as close to anyone as she did to him then.

'I just want to love you,' he breathed, combing his fingers through her hair and cradling the nape of her neck. 'Just want to stay close like this.'

She knew he meant more than physically—that he felt this emotional connection as profoundly as she.

'Don't ever shut me out.' His eyes gleamed with that contrary mix of arrogance and vulnerability that she now understood and adored in him.

'Never.' Another tear escaped, but her soul eased. 'I'm here for you—you're here for me.'

It really was that simple. That true. That perfect. She had never thought she could ever feel this happy. This loved.

He smiled that gorgeous, dimple-studded smile that was simultaneously wicked and challenging and irresistible and heart-stopping.

'Always.'

EPILOGUE

PRINCE EDUARDO DE SANTIS cradled the tiny baby in his arms and looked across the room at his sleeping wife. She was pale and she had smudges beneath her eyes, and her hair was swept back in a loose, messy ponytail, but he'd never seen her looking so beautiful.

The bells celebrating the birth had only recently stopped ringing across the city. The bells in his heart were still going strong—reverberating with joy around his body. His wife and daughter were well and happy and *safe*. And he'd never felt so lucky. Never so grateful.

'No reason why she couldn't be a non-commissioned officer if she wanted,' he said slowly, turning to the older man who stood in the room with him.

A slow smile spread across General Zambrano's face. 'No reason. She'd be good at training on the base.'

'Part-time is possible, eventually?' Eduardo suggested.

He'd not wanted Stella to work during her pregnancy, and she'd mostly relented in her opposition to that request, accompanying him on outings only when she was feeling well. But now…

He knew she wanted to be the best, most 'there' mother she could be, and he had no doubt that she would be, but he suspected she missed flexing other muscles as well. Attending art exhibition openings with him wasn't going to be enough for her. She needed options.

'Of course. Just one or two classes a week, and she can do them more or less as and when she likes. She was always our fittest female recruit. Beat more than half the men.'

'The strongest of the lot.' Eduardo smiled smugly. And the most determined.

'You know her quite well, then?' The General actually winked.

'Getting there.' He was going to need the rest of his life to *really* get to know her.

'Don't think you're going to make plans for my future without letting *me* have a say in it.'

A cool voice from the corner made Eduardo turn back towards the bed. His heart soared when he saw the glint in Stella's eyes.

'You're awake.' He stated the obvious with the smile she always pulled from him—from the deepest corner of his heart.

'Of course I am,' she answered sweetly. 'I've been awake the last five minutes, eavesdropping on you two cooing over our baby.'

Even her father let out a rare laugh. 'Then you know I'm late getting back to my office already.'

'Shocking behaviour for a general,' she admonished him. 'But utterly appropriate for a father and brand-new grandfather.'

Eduardo glanced at the older man and saw the softness in his eyes. And the concern.

'Now I've seen you awake and well...' her father began.

'I'm fine, Dad. Stand down. Go.' She reassured him and released him, with a smile that held just a hint of vulnerability. 'I love you,' she said softly.

'I love you too,' her father mumbled, gruff and swift, and he was out of the room before he'd even finished the garbled words.

With a chuckle, Eduardo carried his daughter over to her mother. 'He's getting better at it,' he teased. 'And so are you.'

That she'd gone through most of her life without being told that she was loved still broke his heart. So he made it his business to tell her every day. Several times a day. And he liked to show her too—every way he could think of.

'I'm making him practise all the time.' Stella glanced

from the door her father had just walked out of back to him. 'Eventually it'll come naturally, right?'

That was his Stella. Brave and honest and always trying so very hard.

'He dotes on his granddaughter already.' Eduardo carefully passed their sleeping baby to her. 'I had to prise her from his arms before.'

'Really?'

A happy glow lit her eyes, making the blue that touch more vibrant. He could look into those eyes for ever.

'You're not just finessing that?'

He shook his head. 'He adores her. Just as he adores you.' He kissed her. 'Just as *I* adore you.'

He sat back and drank in the sight of Stella cradling their stirring baby. Loved and loving, she was indescribably beautiful.

'Antonio had to leave a while ago.' He cleared the huskiness from his throat. 'An issue has come up.'

'Of course.' Stella half-sighed, half-laughed. 'I wish he wasn't so alone. It doesn't seem fair when we have everything.'

'We're here for him,' Eduardo muttered. 'A whole little back-up team now. You never know. He might even loosen up and hold her one day.'

Stella adjusted her robe to nurse her daughter, unable to believe that this tiny piece of perfection was hers. That she and Eduardo had created her.

Princess Sapphira Rose Alessia was almost twelve hours old. They'd named her for the stone that symbolised so much for them, and to break with the tradition that she'd been born into. Sapphira would be *herself.* And then, out of love, they'd honoured Stella's mother, Rose, and Antonio's fiancée, Alessia.

Crown Prince Antonio had taken that news with the tiniest flicker of tension in one eyelid—which Stella had taken to mean that he was deeply touched. He'd just never show it more than that.

In the six months since she'd married Eduardo her life had been transformed. They'd shared so much. She'd gone to every royal engagement of his that she could—both official and unofficial. He'd trained with her, helping her adjust her activities as her pregnancy had progressed. And he'd gone to every medical appointment with her. They'd talked through secrets and fears, they'd joked and battled in board games, they'd sailed and swum…and they had become more than a partnership. They'd become a *force*.

Yet even now she struggled to believe she was married to this most gorgeous man, who was arrogant and kind and impulsive and so loving.

When the tiny Princess had fallen asleep again he took her and settled her in the beautiful bassinet. Stella's eyes filled as she looked at the tall, loyal man who was such a loving father to their child. And a tender, wicked lover to her.

He turned and caught her emotional moment. In a heartbeat he was beside her, pulling her into his arms, drawing her to rest her head on his shoulder. Her heart melted all over again.

'Heaven on earth,' she mumbled, and felt his grunt of amusement.

'Despite the aches and pains?'

'She was worth it.' She laced her fingers through his, remembering Eduardo's anxiety when she'd gone into labour.

'It happened so fast. I was scared,' Eduardo said huskily.

'Like our marriage.' She gave a watery-eyed chuckle. 'It must be in the blood—she'll be just like you. A pirate princess, swooping in and taking what she wants like *that*.' She snapped her fingers.

'As if *you* don't do exactly the same.' He smiled back. 'She may still be the Crown Princess one day,' Eduardo added, a touch of apology in his tone.

'Maybe.' Stella nodded. Given Antonio's frozen heart, it seemed likely. 'But she'll definitely be queen of her own destiny.'

With a laugh Eduardo leaned forward and kissed her. She

kissed him back so ardently he groaned. 'How soon till I can take you both home?'

'My pirate has no patience,' she teased, but she was pleased.

'Do you blame me for wanting to hoard my precious treasure and keep it all to myself?'

He was never going to be able to do that—at least, not for long. There'd be photo calls and royal duty and responsibility soon enough. But there would also be their tiny island to escape to, with its beautiful palace and its secret cave and the wealth of treasures that both contained—the memories they'd already made and the moments that were yet to come.

Stella gazed at her husband and that old familiar tightness gripped her throat. But she pushed past it anyway. 'I love you. Beyond words. Beyond everything.'

'I love you too.'

He cupped her face tenderly and gave her a look that told her everything she'd always wanted to hear: that she had everything she'd wanted to have.

'For ever and always.'

* * * * *

COMING NEXT MONTH FROM
HARLEQUIN
Presents

Available March 15, 2016

#3417 THE SICILIAN'S STOLEN SON
by Lynne Graham
Jemima Barber promised to look after her troubled late twin sister's son. So when the boy's father turns up to reclaim the child, Jemima pretends to be her seductress of a sister...until Luciano Vitale discovers she's a virgin!

#3418 THE BILLIONAIRE'S DEFIANT ACQUISITION
by Sharon Kendrick
For Conall Devlin to complete his property portfolio, he's willing to accept an unusual term of the contract...taming his client's wayward daughter! And Conall's plan is to offer Amber Carter her first job—being at his beck and call day and *night*...

#3419 SEDUCED INTO HER BOSS'S SERVICE
by Cathy Williams
When widower Stefano Gunn met Sunny Porter, he was sure of two things—she was the perfect person to take care of his daughter *and* the most sinfully seductive woman he's seen! And in this game of seduction he *will* win...

#3420 ENGAGED TO HER RAVENSDALE ENEMY
The Ravensdale Scandals
by Melanie Milburne
Jasmine Connolly decides to make her ex-fiancé jealous by enlisting the help of her enemy, Jake Ravensdale! But behind their fake relationship tensions build as the line between love and hate increasingly blurs, teetering on the brink of explosion!

HPCNM0316RA

#3421 A DIAMOND DEAL WITH THE GREEK
by Maya Blake

Arabella "Rebel" Daniels would rather skydive naked than agree to Draco Angelis's outrageous suggestion. But, unbeknownst to Rebel, her father embezzled money from the formidable magnate, and now *she* must pay back the debt by whatever method Draco demands!

#3422 INHERITED BY FERRANTI
by Kate Hewitt

It's been seven years since Sierra Rocci left Marco Ferranti on the eve of their convenient wedding. But now that she's back in Sicily, Marco needs Sierra's help with his latest business venture and is determined to claim their wedding night!

#3423 ONE NIGHT TO WEDDING VOWS
by Kim Lawrence

Lara Gray is consumed by the passion awakened within her after one night with Raoul Di Vittorio. But what she doesn't know is that Raoul needs a temporary wife, and he thinks Lara is the ideal woman for the job!

#3424 THE SECRET TO MARRYING MARCHESI
Secret Heirs of Billionaires
by Amanda Cinelli

Read all about Italian billionaire Rigo Marchesi's secret love child with London actress Nicole Duvalle. This bombshell could destroy CEO Rigo's latest business deal. Unless the rumors that the baby scandal will have a fairy-tale ending are true?

Whatever You're Into...

HARLEQUIN® *Desire*

Tomboy Anna Brown *wants* to tap into her
femininity, but is clueless on *how* to do so.
When her brothers bet she'll be dateless at a charity
auction, she turns to a makeover—and her
way-too-sexy best friend—to prove them wrong.

TAKE ME, COWBOY
From the miniseries *Copper Ridge*
by
Maisey Yates

Available April 2016,
wherever books and ebooks are sold!

Also, remember to collect all 6 titles from
Harlequin® Desire every month!

Stay Connected:

www.Harlequin.com

[f] /HarlequinBooks

[t] @HarlequinBooks

[p] /HarlequinBooks

Presents

92 $1.00
BOOK·OFF

How is she going to tell him?

Army lieutenant Stella Zambrano had the surprise of her life when a routine medical check revealed she was pregnant. Tapping into survival mode, the headstrong beauty only has two thoughts on her mind:

1. Knowing she *must* conceal the father's identity.

2. And wondering what it means for the career she worked so hard for?

Because Stella's baby bombshell is the result of one shockingly sensual afternoon on a deserted beach with Prince Eduardo De Santis. And with an out-of-wedlock heir on the cards, Stella knows the playboy prince will demand marriage!

$4.99 U.S./$5.99 CAN.

ISBN-13: 978-0-373-13422-9

50499

CATEGORY
PASSION

H HARLEQUIN
™ PRESENTS®

harlequin.com

9 780373 134229

EAN

S